MW00717562

LADY VICTORY
MONUMENT CIRCLE
INDIANAPOLIS, INDIANA

EDITOR	Robert Stapleton
ASSOCIATE EDITOR	Chris Speckman
COPY EDITOR	Ashley Petry
ART EDITOR	Andrea Boucher
POETRY EDITOR	Caitlin Dicus
FICTION EDITOR	Greg O'Neill
NONFICTION EDITOR	Erin Wythe
INTERVIEWS EDITOR	Ashley Petry
TWITTER BOSS	Susan Lerner

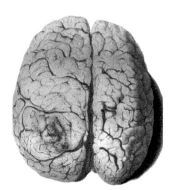

READERS

Stephanie Anderson, Suzie Bartholomew, Kelly Flynn, Connor Kesslering, Luke Purdy, Chris Ryan, Rick Sell, Maggie Sweeney, Samantha Vorwald, Dominique Weldon, Emily Wiland, Nicole Brooks, Hannah Sullivan Brown, Malachi Carter, Natalie Tombasco, Lisa Frazeur, Rae Hudnell, Susan Lerner

Layout and page design by Andrea Boucher.

Copyright © 2017 by Booth and contributors. All rights revert to contributors.

Booth is published biannually in print and weekly online at *booth.butler.edu*.

We accept electronic submissions (only) from September 1 to Marsh 31 at *booth. submittable.com/submit*. Full guidelines on website.

We are grateful for the ongoing support of the Butler University MFA program and the College of Liberal Arts & Sciences at Butler University.

ISBN: 978-0-9906364-5-8
Printed in United States

Visit us online at
booth.butler.edu

CONTENTS

FROM THE EDITOR 7

World, Heaving 12
KRISTA CHRISTENSEN

Suprasellar 25
ANNALISE MABE

Motherlode 30
BRENNA WOMER

How to Write a Rape Piece
(If You Really Feel You Must) 32
KATHERINE Q. STONE

Three Lists 46
MARYA HORNBACHER

12 Letters to the CosmoMutt 54
LIZ N. CLIFT

13 Things Your Mail Carrier
Won't Tell You 58
SARAH LAYDEN

If You and I Said *Fuck It,* and Bought
the Ranch in Montana 62
H. K. HUMMEL

Yesterday's Bestiary for Tomorrow 63
H. K. HUMMEL

Alien Invasions at the
Evans Salvage Grocery 65
M. D. MYERS

[If you said *kitchen* and meant *harden* and
then if you walked out back and forgot] 67
KALLIE FALANDAYS

Orbit 68
HELENA CHUNG

In Defense of Being the Other Woman 71
SARAH DALTON

Poem Where I Almost Hit a Coyote 72
ARIANE SANDFORD

Calling Her Names 74
STEVIE EDWARDS

After Party 76
STEVIE EDWARDS

lawn mower one 79
BETSY JOHNSON-MILLER

Tita 82
MELISSA LLANES BROWNLEE & SEAN MARMON

A Girl Is (Not) a Pirate Ship 93
ERIN KATE RYAN

Dear Nobody 97
KIRSTY LOGAN

Cliffs of Tojinbo 101
CATHY ULRICH

Whale Watch Chaperone
Application 17.B 105
KAITLYN ANDREWS-RICE

There Once Was a Man 117
KELCEY PARKER ERVICK

The Giant's Needle 127
ALLISON WYSS

Rehearsed 130
KATIE YOUNG FOSTER

Aftermilk 134
TARA CAMPBELL

My Name Is Kit Tucker
and I Exist in Sound 142
JUSTINE CHAN

Donation 145
COURTNEY CRAGGETT

We Don't Live by the Sea Anymore 149
DEANIE VALLONE

Vacation, Thirty-Three 153
CADY VISHNIAC

Afterbirth 154
AUBREY HIRSCH

A Conversation with Emily St. John Mandel 158
ASHLEY PETRY

A Conversation with Joyce Carol Oates 171
SUSAN LERNER

A Conversation with Brenda Shaughnessy 179
NATALIE LOUISE TOMBASCO

A Conversation with Elizabeth Strout 191
SAMANTHA VORWALD

A Conversation with Meghan Daum 199
SUSAN LERNER

CONTRIBUTORS 217

FROM THE EDITOR

In April of 2015, after announcing the ten shortlisted poems for that year's *Booth* Poetry Prize, we received the following email:

From: J____
Sent: Saturday, April 11, 2015 6:23 PM
To: BOOTH
Subject: Re: Booth Poetry Contest

Eight of your ten finalists are women. Is this gender bias or chance?

I tried to keep my cool and wrote the following response: "We read the longlist of fifty poems without names, so none of us had any idea. But considering the deeply troubling reality of male-slanted writers and reviewers in American letters today (do you keep up with the annual VIDA count?), I am perfectly fine with our ratio." My reply ended the correspondence with frustrated male writer, but it did not end my relationship to his inquiry.

*

Last spring I taught a course titled "Literary Editing & Publishing" in Butler's MFA program. As part of the curriculum, I ask the students to register a four-issue subscription to the Journal of the Month's classroom program. I select ahead of time the titles, and then the program ships out those issues every month. This time we read *Conjunctions, The Gettysburg Review, A Public Space,* and *Prairie Schooner.* I'm not making news by writing that literary magazines, generally speaking, continue to be a space where writers of some privilege meditate on their circumstances while writers of less privilege appear less often—and with different kinds of narratives. This is not true at all for *A Public Space,* and also not true for many sharp and thoughtful selections from any of the titles above. And frankly, the same can be said for *Booth;* the struggle to represent more diverse voices and broader experiences relies powerfully on the kinds of submissions we receive. But as a professor responsible for shaping and re-shaping the canon, I was reminded of the homogeneity of literary magazines while discussing the contemporary work in these issues.

When work submitted to *Booth* passes successfully through reading teams and goes up the ladder to our monthly roundtable, we remove the names for discussion and voting. Sometimes an author's gender is seemingly apparent from the work and other times a complete mystery. Either way, when there's twenty of us in a room debating, we don't give it much truck. We are in dogged pursuit of the best material we can find to publish.

Once accepted, work appears on our website.[1] Roughly twice a year, we curate print issues from the material that we've published online. And we never develop print issues without keeping a running count of the female/male ratio. In our recent 450-page anniversary issue, *Booth X,* we included thirty-two female authors and thirty-eight male authors. In *Booth 9,* the ratio was 12/12. We believe in the VIDA count as a critical cultural barometer of whose voices find airtime, and until VIDA includes us in their pie charts, we will hold ourselves accountable to the notion there is a multiplicity of important and arresting voices in the world. We are committed to being as inclusive as possible.

*

We received work from around five-hundred poets during the prize gig mentioned above. Our poetry editor that year was Kaveh Akbar. He was an amazingly dedicated editor who sifted through submissions in a thoughtful manner and at an impressive rate. He brought us the fifty longlisted poems, sans author names, and three of us sat down to put some debate to the matter. I'm not proud to say that all three editors at the table were male, but I am proud to say that we have had an abundance of incredible, female editors both before and after that afternoon.[2] To the

---

[1] In 2016, we published on our website work from twenty-three female authors and twenty-five male authors. In the first half of 2017, we have published work from seventeen female authors and nine male authors.

[2] Specifically, twelve of twenty-one Booth editor positions have been held by women since the poetry contest. In the interest of full disclosure, before this email arrived at headquarters, Booth's female/male editor ratio was 17/33.

best of my memory, we never gave a second thought to the possible gender identities of the ten shortlisted poems. The final judge was Ellen Bryant Voigt; the *Booth* staff sat down with her a few weeks later, and she shared much wisdom about all ten poems before selecting Paula Brancato's "The only time I ever cried at the gym."

*

The idea for an issue of *Booth* dedicated to all women writers arrived while leading discussion of other lit mags in my editing course this past spring. And every time I looked at our list of recent acceptances and began to pull together a possible list of female authors, I'd stumble across so many amazing pieces we'd accepted by men who were, and still are, rightfully waiting to appear in print. And I'd get conflicted for a minute that we were asking these men to wait. But, you know, that concern quickly passed. American history is dominated by the patience of women, and the world of American publishing, a garden of so much culture and progressive thought, should have been leading this charge long ago. Furthermore, if you are a male writer and take umbrage that we would put together this issue, no matter how accomplished your work, I'd ask you to not submit to us in the future. I'm not suggesting we need to share the same politics for you to appear in *Booth*, but I am suggesting you should understand that our interest in publishing dynamic literature intersects with our interest in publishing the multiplicity of voices in the full breadth of our shared, contemporary experience.

*

Finally, I'd like to dedicate this issue of *Booth* to the author of the April 2015 inquiry above, J_____. Without his email, *Booth 11: Women Writers* would probably not exist. Your legacy is greater than you know.

Robert Stapleton

nonfiction

World, Heaving

KRISTA CHRISTENSEN

"For now truly is a race of iron, and men never rest from labour and sorrow by day, and from perishing by night; and the gods shall lay sore trouble upon them."

—Hesiod, *Works and Days*
tran. Hugh Evelyn-White

IN ALASKA, AUTUMN HAS A special name: September.

On the fourth day of this single-month season, the sun hangs antithetically high in the evening sky, still and yellow and cool. The late-coming tourists are out. This is how we speak of visitors in Alaska, that they are "out" in the same way that the moon might be "out," which is to say that they are unlikely to be missed and difficult to avoid. Droves of people ring this small grassland, just a few hundred yards in diameter. From the neck of one man, a heavy black Nikon dangles, fully equipped with a lens the length of my forearm. The man occasionally lifts this behemoth to his face and squints in concentration; on a viewing deck, a woman maneuvers her earnest toddler awkwardly up to the mounted binoculars. When the toddler pulls his face away, his eyes are ringed, raccoon-like, from pressing his chubby face against the lenses—from his efforts to see what there is to see.

My guess is he sees nothing but darkness. Nonetheless, he is appeased.

They are here for the birds: this field is a major stop-off for migratory waterfowl, all heading due south, away from the snow and ice that will coat the land, and soon—in six weeks or less, and certainly before Halloween. Flocks of Canada geese have descended on the plain, and the mass of black and white feathers is punctuated by the tall taupe figures of sandhill cranes, who on their stick legs seem to strut haughtily around and between their squat, goose-y companions with their waggling hind ends. At a distance of fifty yards, hundreds of feathered bodies wriggle over and under one another, and all I can conjure is a swarm of bees, or a litter of new blind mammals, mewling.

And fertilizer. Lots of that will be left behind.

I moved to Alaska for the second time a few weeks ago, having taken a job teaching here (for the second time), partly for the stout paycheck and partly because I missed the extremity of it all—the boundary-pushing, oxymoronic twin senses of excess and privation. Nonetheless, my hours this early September have been spent almost entirely indoors. My classroom, because I am new to the district and low in seniority, is windowless, so that even though I have come to the land of midnight sun a full month before the equinox, I am not a party to the long days happening beyond the thick walls of the school building.

So on I march, past the Nikon man and his many twins, and at the end of the field loop trail, I duck into the shade of trees, slipping away from the birds and their audience and into the forest. This is the Interior of Alaska, the heart of the Taiga, the boreal forest that today makes up the largest land biome in the world, where stands of birch and scatterings of spruce and tamarack form a cocoon, a protective coating buffering me from the squawking of birds and people. The allure of migration means that this loop of the nature preserve will be nearly empty. I'm happy about that.

The birch have, even now in the first week of September, begun to glow, ember-like, their limbs trimmed in shimmery gold leaves, although August is not five days into history. At their feet, rose hips ripen, and these leaves of wild rose bushes glare a deepening red, so that the forest appears fiery, sunk in a season of sun going down—quickly, at the rate of seven minutes per day—in flames. The trail transitions to a wooden boardwalk, transporting me across a body of water I persist (it turns out, incorrectly) in calling a slough because it harbors, each warm season, the runoff of meltwater from the previous winter. Helpfully, a sign farther up the trail informs me that this is, instead, a thermokarst pond, meltwater swelling seasonally on blunted land—former permafrost that thawed during a wildfire, causing firm soil to sink and bulge in unexpected places before refreezing again and again each winter. From my place on the boardwalk, I take in a vista of drunken trees across the still water, a tilted grove of spindly birches decked in white paper and the gold of a northern autumn. These are interspersed with stubby black spruce, all upcurved arms that appear always to be shrugging, unsure of their place in the way of things but smirking nonetheless.

One of every five trees, I estimate, lists heavily at an odd, intersecting angle, giving the whole forest a chaotic, prickly feel. The boardwalk is tilting and shifting beneath my feet—imperceptibly at first, but as I delve deeper into the woods, the angle of the planks grows intense, forty-five degrees or more in some places, and abruptly the tilt of the trees becomes acute, not simply in the mathematical sense of less than a right angle, but in the medical sense of severity, of highly problematic, of approaching life-threatening. Certain birches duck so low that their gold leaves are swallowed by the mucky water, still and greenish and topped with float-ing leaves and lily pads and opaque films that swirl hypnotically. I pass a toppled tree's massive root ball; it lies prone before me, exposed, a gaping hole yawning below where it overturned, the whole business naked in a spread-eagled way. Its splayed essence reminds me of gynecological exams.

Three-quarters of a mile in, the boardwalk's listing reaches critical mass, and my feet slide down the planks where the left half of the boardwalk juts up high and the right dips low, grazing the coated water. The bridge is toppling by seasons, one centimeter at a time. I steady my steps with a hand on the nearest birch—another listing tree, it and the boardwalk both products of this heaving world of freeze and thaw, its mud-colored under-trunk tacky where the papery outer layers have been peeled clean, like many birches here, by moose yearlings higher up, by snowshoe hares lower down.

Here, in the subarctic, life is lived by degrees. The leaning trees mirror the tilt of the world's axis, the serendipitous geophysical phenomenon that bestows on us not only the birch's gold profusion but also the bounty of seasonal agriculture in general, the wobbliness of the world a blessing upon which we all depend. The very earth here is a harbinger of constant change; it shifts perpetually, a dynamic system that protests being pinned down by roadways and building foundations. Thawed ground freezes, iron hard, in the deep of winter, swelling up as if inflated from beneath, only to deflate, like an empty balloon, at spring's thaw. Frost heaves, these are called. I marvel at how their behavior mimics breathing, that constant swelling and deflating of existence. Their cycles of melt and freeze, of soft and firm, of pliability and resistance, produce ever-shifting mounds of earth, and it is this that fascinates me: the instability of what is seemingly stable, the contradictory nature of life in the far north, where the oscillating seasons, each in their turn, deliver abundance and punish absolutely.

*

THE birch, like the tilted world, is a deceptively modest source of abundance. For so long, Athabaskans and northerners have tapped birch sap for boiling into syrup, much like maples are tapped on the other side of the continent. They have skinned the birch in the early spring, carefully harvesting the bark in great sheets that they sewed over canoe frames, crafting vessels worthy of rivers as wide and mighty as the Yukon and Tanana, while from smaller swatches of spring-harvested bark they sewed bowls of various sizes. All this they did using bone-carved awls for pilot-

ing holes, green high cranberry-bush switches for rims, and moose hide or threaded spruce roots for sewing. Like their canoe cousins, birch bowls are water-tight; even without cookpots (or sewing needles), Athabaskans used these bowls to cook moose, hare, squirrel, and more by heating stones in fires and placing the hot stones in birch bowls with water and strips of flesh. The conducted heat coaxed the water to boiling, and the flesh into food. Soaked bark bowls, among other tools, also served to transport smoldering coals, giving the people easy access to a warm fire throughout winter travel between camps.

What Athabaskans achieved with this one simple resource is truly marvelous, a word I do not employ lightly: the birch bark bowl I have held in my hands is a baffling wonder of human skill and ingenuity. I can produce nothing so significant, for it is a product squarely residing at the intersection of form and function, of use and beauty. Even so, all this business, from bowls to boats, is crafted with what humans in many places consider Stone Age technology—as in, fashioned without metal tools or supplies.

Stone Age. The notion itself is a wholly Eurocentric concept. The Association of Social Anthropologists has long issued edicts insisting that references to people as "Stone Age" and "primitive" are inappropriate. Institutional mandates cannot eradicate these stereotypes, which nonetheless persist. The generally accepted end to the Stone Age (and humanity's corresponding entrance into the age of metalworking) is between 8,000 and 2,000 BCE. This dovetails with the time that humans in today's Eastern Europe and northern Near East began extracting copper from the Zagros and Taurus mountains. Yet archeological evidence shows Athabaskans did not begin metalworking in the Copper River Delta until about a thousand years ago.

Contemporary Westerners have the habit of lauding such "Stone Age" artifacts for their beauty and usefulness with a spectator's awe, impressed at how people managed to create such a thing in spite of their supposedly limited technology. This is a common landing area for the indigenous narrative in the hands of Western history: a place of awe contaminated with a subversive—and pervasive—pity, or at the very least some backhanded acknowledgement of lack, a perpetual reminding that, while these people made amazing objects and survived well and adapted to harsh conditions and maintained complicated social and cultural structures and struggled with the same existential questions we all do, they nonetheless did it *without* ————. This, at its core, is a presumption that these societies were somehow incomplete until "advanced" Westerners arrived, bringing whatever fill-in-the-blank they deemed necessary to bring "primitives" out of their dark Stone Age.

Think of the great care taken to record archaeological and anthropological locations and details: the first instances of primates using tools, the first evidence of quarrying and mining, the first appearance of metalwork, of shaping and smithing. Indeed, the notion of Western ancient history completely centers on the progression of humanity through ages of increasing complexity. The assumption is that making things more complicated inherently improves a people's success and wellbeing. Sometimes that's the case, I suppose; sometimes not. Nonetheless, this focus on "progress" and forward momentum has a tendency to portray human history as a wobbling yearling, one before which we twenty-first-century-ists sit, clapping and cooing encouragements at each toddling step that "primitives" make toward "progress." Even pointing out the date at which the Athabaskans began working with copper gives a sense, still, that they are somehow behind their peers, as if they were children held back in school.

But was the move out of a hunter-gatherer social structure a leap forward, rather than a change of course? Why are mining and smelting ore considered the hallmarks of human progress? This seems like an arbitrary point of development at best, and a contentious one at worst. Indeed, what was lost in the transition from barter systems to coin currencies? What was traded for the advances of gunpowder and broadswords? What sprang loose in the human heart at the advent of gold and silver and shining treasures? For all the children protected by vaccines we have traded the children dead of miners' black lung disease. For today's smartphones we have traded black children in the Congo mining coltan. For the convenience of speedy travel we have traded oceans slicked with spilled oil and gyres of accumulated plastic offal. For the safety and comfort of indoor plumbing, we have traded cyanide-laced water tables in the vicinity of open-pit mines.

These last two matter a lot, especially here in the Arctic. Gold is what brought Americans here in the first place, after the Russians had all but decimated small mammal populations in their fur trade (and I use the term trade loosely). Now Alaska is home to six very large mines that extract mostly gold but also zinc, copper, and other minerals, such as molybdenum. The land is peppered, too, with prospects: more than seventy-five of them active, each a potential mine in itself, and dozens more abandoned, now nothing more noble or useful than a gaping maw of hungry earth.

Fort Knox, an active open-pit gold mine, lies twenty-six miles northeast of where I stand now, surveying my tilted birches and listing boardwalk and scummy water, where the squawks of birds and their watchers are mere echoes, where you'd never know by the lifted sun that the time nears nine at night. And close by there is, too, that other product of holes drilled in earth, the black gold oozing through it at the rate of a million dollars an hour. It's just eight miles away: the Trans-Alaska Pipeline, snaking south to Valdez, a place synonymous with oil and disaster, down from Prudhoe Bay on the Arctic Ocean, where no fewer than sixteen rigs hover on icy sea and sand in the largest petroleum reserve in North America.

See how they speckle the land, all these punctures, these wounds in the earth. Out of them spill valuables, costly treasures that she surrenders, and after, when the earth is spent, when the hole has been thoroughly routed, she is abandoned. Where the pounding and thrusting and drilling and excavating took place, only the empty shaft is left, a window into this unstable, shifting ground, a gap in land that thaws and refreezes violently, uprooting trees and buckling roadways and crumpling foundations—a land literally heaving.

For most of us, though, opposition to mining is terribly hypocritical. The industry fuels the Alaskan economy in tangible ways: funding road repairs, for instance, which are constantly necessary given the swell and ebb of ice beneath the ground (or rather, given that automobiles are a wholly unsuitable mode of travel in the Arctic). It gets personal, too. I use a smartphone, I wear a wedding ring, I cook in stainless steel, I own a refrigerator and a car and lots and lots of cheap jewelry. And each evening, the incandescent (or, more likely, compact fluorescent) glow of lamps in my home and on my street comes at the cost of coal mined 118 miles southwest, at Usibelli; 37 miles west of that coal mine is Mount Denali, the highest point in North America, a place surrounded by an eponymous national park and preserve. Yet none on my street hesitate to flip their light switches, and all around lighted windows become beacons in the black of long northern nights.

The children of gold-mine employees fill the school at which I am a teacher; our town is, as one child so eloquently put it, a place where minors become miners. Here, too, are the children of North Slope oilmen and women who work two or three weeks at a stretch, laboring in bitter cold so cars can run and water can flow and light can beam into the perpetual Alaskan dark. These people, whom we affectionately dub "Slopers," are hardworking and generous, as are the miners. They work long, thankless hours to provide the best for their families and communities. They love the outdoors, love to hunt and fish, and, I must add, follow environmental regulations for both activities diligently. Many are conservationists, and almost all are far more knowledgeable about survival in this harsh landscape than I will ever be. Mining and oil drilling, as industries go, give blue-collar rural families substantial economic advantages.

Still. Nothing is without its costs.

In the last half of the eighth century BCE, Hesiod, a successor to Homer, laid out a theory of man—one that is in every way the reverse of ours—in his *Works and Days.* For him, humanity was engaged not in a progression but in a degradation, an ever-widening chasm between the glory and perfection of the age of the gods and the hard, heavy labor that characterizes the age of men—a perpetual fall from grace, an everlasting delve into the worst aspects of human nature. "The father will not agree with his children," he wrote, "nor the children with their father, nor guest with his host, nor comrade with comrade; nor will brother be dear to brother as aforetime . . . Strength will be right and reverence will cease to be." An epoch, it appears, culminating in might-makes-right. A perennial season of ingratitude, of selfishness, of willfulness and longing and envy and pain. A time quantified by gain, by means and not by ends, by cleverness rather than kindness. And now, in the past fifty years—the past twenty years, the past ten—we have ushered in a new age, one dubbed the "age of information." What progress have we made? Have we leapt forward, or away?

Toward what do we collectively turn our faces?

In the 1950s—during the birth pangs of the information era—Enrico Fermi defined an astrophysical paradox about alien life. He computed, in numbers so enormous I cannot replicate them here, that the odds of intelligent life in our "local group," our neighborhood in the Milky Way galaxy (an area roughly ten million light years wide) was far from impossible. He postulated, in fact, that intelligent life in the universe—based on sheer massive odds—must exist. Yet we have met exactly none; thus the paradox. Recently, physicist Brian Cox posed a solution to the Fermi quandary, and it is this: that a race of beings with the capacity for interstellar travel will, by default, annihilate itself before establishing successful settlements on distant planets, for any group of beings smart enough to develop such technology will collapse before achieving it. The power to colonize other worlds is also the power to destroy one's own. This goes for those who would seek us, and for those whom we would seek.

The theory is simple, then: intelligence predicates extinction.

I wonder whether these theoretical alien civilizations anticipated their apocalypse or whether their lives continued, as ours do, in a merry, distracted way, eyes on the everyday, meandering through a life of constant progress, until suddenly life wasn't anymore. Did everything go in a flash, or did they die slowly, by degrees? I wonder how it was with them in their demise. Did they see it coming and try to avoid the inevitable? Or were they vibrant and happy, right up to the end?

*

September, our sole autumnal month in the far north, is ending, and I have returned to the trees. The first frost of winter settled last night, September 28, and this morning the ice was thick enough for a scraper. A year ago today, people woke to seventeen inches of fresh snowfall; this afternoon, the roads lay frigid yet bare. It has been three weeks since last I walked here: three weeks of work in my windowless classroom; three weeks of papers graded and calls placed and meetings attended; three weeks of increasingly dark commutes and on-time dinners and squealing alarm clocks.

The field is empty now of birds and birders alike; all the geese and sandhill cranes are halfway to Texas, and this afternoon, though it is still high in the sky, the sun hides behind massive clouds, gray and pregnant and fierce. Now is a time of retraction, of breath sucked in and held, abs clenched in anticipation of the gut-punch that is winter in the far north. All my birches are bare now. Three weeks ago, a halo of golden leaves trembled overhead, and now those same leaves paper the walking trail, their evaporated life crunching and squishing by turns on the boardwalk beneath my boots. I pass into the forest and pause, as I have before, inhaling the tableau of crooked, tilting trees and disturbing a lone flock of ducks whose leader issues me noisy remonstrations. Soon, they too are gone—winging off to warmer climes, I hope. I move through expired bulrushes, a late-autumn sludge staining the hem of my skirt. Where before I was caught unaware of the tilts and slants of the earth and its proxy, the boardwalk, I now steady myself on birches here and there. I pass my upturned root ball, that fallen tree hyper-exposed, and ponder, again, the violated scene, mull once more the parallels between the holes made in earth and those born from their products, filtered as they are through engines and generators of all kinds. I can't get over it: the gaping soreness of this defeated tree, its draggled roots dangling from the roundness of the trunk's underside, their ratty, torn edges a helpless witness to its sudden demise. For months after, this tree, overturned, will haunt me.

All around me, the world heaves.

Now that the undergrowth, too, has lost its greenery, the forest floor appears more and more a birch graveyard, fallen trunks crisscrossing haphazardly all about, some deflated in decomposition and coated in lichens, some freshly down with their paper still peeling back in a revelatory way. They appear, today more than ever, like fallen soldiers, and I'm taken with the desire to memorialize them, to be for them some Seussian speaker-for-the-trees, to give them, somehow, their proper due. The collapse around me highlights a fault of my own, and I feel responsible for them, in spite of the truth that, contrary to all my moralizing, I am far more Once-ler than Lorax.

I'm not alone in that fact. All along this hike are interpretive signs like the one from my last walk here that corrected me, told me that this was no mere slough, but a thermokarst formation, a house of melted cards, oozing. Farther, past the defeated tree, past all the defeated trees, I meet another sign. It is titled emphatically "Why IS the Forest Collapsing?" The sign gives me a truncated answer—a few sentences beneath the mounted plastic. The issue is so simple, I suppose, that it may be laid out clearly in a two-by-three square of print media.

I learn from this sign that the heaving boardwalk on which I stand was first constructed in 1977, but since 1996 it has needed constant re-routing to accommodate Earth's changing climate. From the sign, I am introduced to the functions of ice wedges, how their underground thawing causes what are mistaken as sinkholes in a land far from limestone; they in essence subvert the permafrost with their impertinent melting. Finally, in small print, speckled with new and old mud, is a logo: ConocoPhillips, the sign's sponsor.

I pause here, smirking at the irony that this sign, the one explaining the effects of global warming on this particular forest, is sponsored by a purveyor of fuel responsible for the rise in greenhouse gas emissions. But this—the melting ice wedges and thawing permafrost beneath this pond of slanted trees—this is not all ConocoPhillips' fault. It's not all big oil's fault either. Basic economics dictate that a demand will be supplied. Progress marches on. Change is inevitable. There are no false starts in nature, no do-overs allowed. Evolution never runs backward, and it won't ever let us begin afresh, at the first single-celled organism, to see how close to perfection we can come. We must swallow our fuck-ups. And so, I am back at Fermi's paradox, staring at an alien annihilation—ours.

Deeper into the forest, near the end of my walk, I have my eyes on the boardwalk so as not to be taken by surprise at unexpected slants and heaves. Among the decomposing birch leaves at my feet I catch a glint of yellow, bright and out of place: sawdust, I finally surmise, and look up. A few feet ahead, I am confronted by a freshly sawn stump. A particularly tilted birch has been sacrificed, I see, to the gods of the heaving world, mown down in the prime of a life spent leaning, present though off-kilter, crooked but surviving. How like the birch are we, I think: pushing on into unusual territory, listing but making do, knowing things aren't as they should be but pressing forward nonetheless, leaning into progress as if it were the natural way of things. I marvel, up close, at the fresh wood, so brilliant at the point of severance, with such distinct rings that show, clearly, how very alive the tree was—right up to the end.

Suprasellar

ANNALISE MABE

ONTHS AFTER THEY FOUND IT, they still couldn't figure out what it was. My mother consulted with a group of doctors at Johns Hopkins, who told her that I won the award for longest debate over a brain tumor. I imagined them all gathered like ancient Roman astrologers staking out their claims about space. About stars. But instead of a star, it was my brain up on the screen. Its gray folds, tight around a mass sitting square in the middle of my brain. Perfectly spherical.

No one could agree because it didn't look like anything they knew.

"I want to take it out," someone said. "Let's see a piece of it." But in the end they resolved not to touch it. Unless it started to grow.

*

I thought the word suprasellar sounded shiny. It sounded like it could mean super, above, or spectacular, like faraway galaxies or a superhero who could fly through space. A part of me wanted it to mean these things, but it actually just signifies a location, like coordinates for a map. It doesn't actually mean anything. It's simply used to convey information, specifically about where a tumor may live.

*

IT started with headaches. I'm not sure when exactly, but I remember climbing the wooden ladder to my loft bed at my father's house, my hair sopping wet from the shower, soaking into the neck of my t-shirt. I remember my father coming in to say goodnight, turning on my starry night light, patting me on my head that had been aching for hours, pulsing with a new pain. I remember that the pain lived behind my eyes and beneath my cheekbones, stretching tight around my skull, making me need the darkness like I needed water or sleep.

I faced the wall of my bedroom at his lakehouse before he turned off the lights, before the warm orange pulse grew bright and sharp beneath my face, branching out like bean sprouts, or the limbs of a constellation.

*

WHEN I was little, I wondered whether my emotions had legs. I mean that, sometimes they felt so strong, it was as if they were growing into monstrous beings of their own. Sometimes I swore I could feel them. Strong muscly things, knotting in the pit of my stomach. Spreading out their arms like wings, the fringing tips reaching through all of my veins, even to my brain.

*

I wasn't worried about the brain tumor. It didn't scare me because I was eighteen and more concerned about losing my long hair if I had to have brain surgery. One neurosurgeon suggested we go through the nose, which I quickly agreed to, though it never happened.

I wanted to see it, too.

Eighteen is a galaxy of its own: intertwined like the nerve bundles, the brain folds, from which the tumor itself grew. I was with my friends, driving around at night, screaming lyrics with the windows down. Ordering food through the drive-thru. Stopping to wander on wood planks, through mangroves, to a dock on the lake. The water, so black it would swallow us if we fell in. We drank beer from green bottles pulled out of our backpacks. We lay on our backs, and we laughed, looking up at the stars, trying to keep track of the ones we counted and the ones still left to go.

*

BEFORE the tumor, when the tumor was only a headache that doctors didn't know what to do with, there were many migraine pills. Some of them looked like candy: a small pink triangle, a blue enclosed capsule. I tried each one they gave me, often feeling the same effects. Simultaneously, my heart raced and I felt so sleepy. I wanted to close my eyes and sprint at the same time. To clean my room, to put every piece of it back in its place, and also to curl up in the bean bag chair in the corner. I was weary and strong. Weak and energetic. The inconsistency made me drunk, and quiet, waning with still watchful eyes, not wanting to move a muscle. Part of me loved the feeling of floating through hallways. Levitating. My head in a cloud. The other part was afraid, or curious, of what might happen if I couldn't come back down.

*

AS I lay on the clean, robotic table of the MRI machine, the nurse adjusted a plastic cage around my head like a helmet, screwing me in with large radio-jockey headphones. "I'll be right in there," she said, pointing to a glass-walled room. She pressed a button, zooming me into the machine's belly.

I could no longer see her once I was inside, but I heard her voice, crackling through the headphones, soft over the classical music ebbing through the wires. I stared at the machine's spherical walls. Its insides. Loud shudders *onged* out, vibrating my skull like laser tag. Like taking off into outer space, the nurse my mission control in the safe-walled room.

The sharp utterances of the machine boomeranged around my head above the violins stringing quietly, the peaks shrill like the surges bolting through my head. I imagined I was leaving, landing in unknown territory.

The nurse slid me out for a contrast injection, swabbing the inside of my elbow, the skin so thin and nearly translucent. My body cringed at the prick and the pump of cold chemicals into my veins. She zoomed me back in, and this time I closed my eyes. I imagined the swirl of colors entering my bloodstream, a new type of neon that glowed in the dark. Bright and chalky and lifting me up.

ONE of the doctors said it could have been a suprasellar cistern filled with cerebrospinal fluid, or blood from a hemorrhage. A fall, or trauma to the head. Typically, these are shaped like a pentagon or six-pointed star, often likened to the Star of David, known in Hebrew as the Shield. Mine, though, wasn't a star, nor was it a symbolic shield. It wasn't ruled out as good or bad, but simply unknown.

*

THE doctor's report was filled with words I didn't know: ventricles, midline structures, optic chiasm. Parts of my brain that held no meaning for me. Distant places that had lain dormant in me until then. I only understood the word mass. And I saw it on the scan. Perfectly spherical, like a gumball. I wondered what color it would be. A kid with a quarter, waiting for the ball to drop down the spiral of the machine, rolling into the palm of my open hand.

*

PEOPLE can tell when I have a headache. What's wrong? they ask. Migraine? I guess, I say. My headaches were never classified as migraines, but sometimes I tell them yes, just to simplify things. People don't like things that can't be explained. People like for their brains to work less, for answers to come easy. Categories can be helpful. Cutting down on the brain energy used.

But some things cannot be parsed, strained, or separated. There is no mental shortcut for what lives inside of me.

*

OFTEN when I sat in the patient rooms, my mother and the doctors talked, static before me, a TV left on. I took to memorizing the anatomy posters, tracing my eyes over the veins and through the various organs in the belly. Nearly everything had a name, except for the brain. Here, all of the parts were the same gray, indistinguishable like a lump of clay. An emptiness still waiting to be explored or excavated.

*

I still don't know what lives in my brain, what it's made of, or where it came from. Sometimes it seems alien, or even non-existent. Distant and embedded within me at the same time. I know of its location. Its volume. That it sits on the pituitary, right under the intersection where the nerves of my eyeballs cross. I know that if it grows it can touch things, has the potential to render me blind.

I want to know it the same way I've come to know the landscape of my skin. I want to touch it, and to press it between my fingers. I wonder if it would pop or if it would be solid. If it will grow now, or soon, or never. If it will stay asleep, a hibernating star, a ticking time bomb between synaptic flashes, politely minding the gap.

I know that I can't know.

There are many things I cannot know.

I can imagine, though. Breaking it open, its insides flying out. A supernova exploding in silence. Or maybe like machinery, with chunking debris? A flash of light in the sky, a quickening across stars. My eyes widening, waiting for the stop of a hum.

Motherlode

BRENNA WOMER

I WANT TO BE A MOTHER but only on Sundays, yelling at them not to dirty their best in the woods behind the church. French Roast Folgers, Styrofoam cups, single serving Coffee-mate creamers, and Sweet'N Low packets that cause cancer like microwaves and cellphones, but we use them anyway because God is in control. I layer Oreo crumbs, Jell-O pudding, and Cool Whip in hand-me-down Pyrex for the potluck after second service. Don't doodle in the hymnal; shirttail tucked; eyes closed when we pray; take the grape juice from the inner circle—the wine is for Mommy; don't eat the bread, the body, before Pastor blesses it.

I want to be a mother when she has ballet at the little studio downtown; when his number is painted on my cheek for Friday night football; during the hour we spend making brownies and then licking the bowl, and in the thirty seconds it takes them to tear through their Christmas Eve stockings.

I want to be a mother, but only during the in-between times when I'm not fucking it up. When I'm not giving them a reason to hate me, hate the world, hate themselves. Early on, when they're fresh things, in those quiet night hours as they feed from my body, looking at me or past me—my connection to the realm of spirits, to God the Father, the Mother. My portal to a higher, better place before they learn to be here, to be human.

I want to be a mother before my daughter learns what she is to the world, before she gets angry at me for telling her the way things are, for breaking that beautiful spell as my own mother did. Before she spreads her legs for the first, the could-be, the why-won't-you, the true, the broken, and the anything-to-fill-this-hole kinds of love. We are not princesses.

I want to be a mother before I hate my son for what's between his legs: the soft, pillowy flesh he'll learn to wield like a sword. Let me be a mother before he realizes the power he has. Before boys will be boys and all guys do it and that's just the way men are. When he's brand new and sliding out of me, when he's latched on and drinking, when he bathes with his sister and kisses her on the mouth—before the world teaches them their place.

I want to be a mother, because I'm supposed to want to be a mother. But as I sat waiting for the nurse to come back with pregnancy-test results, a picture of two kids in a cornfield taped to her name badge, it wasn't a choice. It wasn't want. It was a thing that was happening, like an earthquake or daylight saving time. And even if I decided to say No, no thank you or Not now, not yet—even if I slept through the quake and refused to set my clocks back—still, forever, once, I was a mother. I was the one who would love and ruin them, the one they'd respect and blame. I was the one who'd know their bodies first, their minds, before they knew themselves, and keep their secrets before they understood there were any to keep. With a cocktail of fear and want, no and yes, me and all their potential in my belly, I was—for however brief a time—Mother.

How to Write a Rape Piece (If You Really Feel You Must)

KATHERINE Q. STONE

Start with a joke. It makes you more likeable.

I was assaulted while wearing a T-shirt reading "Blondes Have More Fun." Believe me, they didn't have much fun that night.

The joke will not only ease the tension but will also make it clear that you're not one of *those* victims. You're not exactly sold on the term *survivor* either, but at least you're separating yourself from those women who travel from high school to high school, telling their stories and passing out magnets reading "No Means No" because someone told them that the best way to move on from a problem is to talk about it ad nauseam to anyone who will listen. But at least they're getting paid to relive the worst night of their lives a few times a week, while you're doing it every day for free. And, survivor or victim, you were still attacked either way.

Insert a brief anecdote here to make your story even more relatable, to illustrate, once again, how you used to see yourself as above other victims who you think define themselves based on the great tragedies of their lives. How you hated other survivors for defining themselves by something you were able to get past. Of course, if you do this, you won't be as likeable, and half those reading will imme-diately scroll down to the comments section to write something about how you're "obviously still hurting." But at least you'll have painted yourself as a person with a little more depth who, with the benefit of hindsight, is capable of being self-critical in the present.

You remember when the rape crisis counselor, or, as you heard someone call her, the "professional victim," came to your school. You all filed into the auditorium, angry that you weren't having mid-morning break that day. Mid-morning break was when you got your yogurt and granola with strawberries on top, and the only time of the day you got to see the boy you liked. You can't believe you're missing that. Besides, no one here would ever do something like this anyway, so what's the point? The professional victim makes her speech, and a girl from your French class starts crying. She's in the row in front of you, trapped between two members of the football team in the center of the seats, so there's no way for her to get up without the entire school noticing. You're old enough to piece together why she might be crying, but, for whatever reason, it never occurs to you until years later.

You wonder whether you're supposed to clap after a rape speech. You settle on a light tap of the palms, accompanied by an awkward glance to your friends. You feel good that you've escaped, that at least you didn't break down like the girl from your French class did. You are tougher. You are fine now. Then you are separated. The boys stay seated, and the girls get up to walk halfway across campus (of course) so that you can go into even further detail about how *you* can stop yourself from being raped. Do not walk alone at night. Take karate. Avoid dangerous neighborhoods. Do not wear revealing clothing if you must visit a homeless shelter or prison. The session ends with all the girls chanting, "If I am raped, it is not my fault," which seems contradictory to everything the rape prevention team member said. You are then given a caramel candy—your favorite. This makes up for missing mid-morning break. Afterward, in the hallway, you laugh at the boys imitating the professional victim's tears. You laugh be-cause it's safer to. Socially and otherwise. The boys are angry because they say all they got was yelled at, and the girls got candy. They feel this was very unfair.

Quick question: Can you still tell a rape joke if you weren't all-the-way raped?

One of the best things about being sexually assaulted is that suddenly you're allowed to say all kinds of terrible things and call them "empowering" or "part of the process," and nobody, except for other victims (whom you actively avoid), can say anything. Like your classmate who had an abortion and makes it the punch line of every joke. *I can't believe there was a woman in the clinic's waiting room who brought her lunch in a Babies R Us bag.* Of course you laugh, because you have to. To laugh at this kind of joke is to enter into an unspoken agreement with its teller, to accept the challenge of refusing to give something the kind of attention it deserves, to let the teller believe that she has "moved on." You agree to laugh not because it's easier but because it's much harder. Because you desperately want to ask how she's doing, but she desperately needs you to laugh. To cry is something a victim would do. To laugh is the stuff of a survivor. At least that's your excuse.

A friend of yours likes to bring up her rape at dinner parties. It's uncomfortable, but no one can say anything. Once, someone brought up a recent trip to Milan, and she interjected: *Milan. Beautiful city. Did I ever tell you I was raped there?*

Usually, the party ends shortly thereafter.

Rape: The Numbers, or Better You than Me

WHEN writing about rape, it's also advisable to avoid statistics, which have a tendency to scare people. When you hear things like "One in three women will be raped in her lifetime" or "A rape occurs every two minutes in America," you immediately start to think of two women you know and wonder which one of you is going to get raped, which one of you is going to get cancer, and which one of you is going to have a stillbirth (because if you're looking up rape statistics, you might as well check on the cervical cancer and miscarriage ones, too). Or, worse, what if everything happens to the same person? Maybe you did your friends a favor by being the "one in three"; maybe they won't be assaulted because you already took care of it for them. But does this mean you're also going to get cervical cancer? You start to get angry at the injustice of statistics. Should you *really* have to be the one who gets raped *and* gets cervical cancer? How is that fair? These are the kinds of thoughts statistics induce. Besides, you wonder, how accurate can they really be? It's not like women all over the world are foaming at the mouth to complete surveys on sexual assault. Speaking of: While you're reading this, between two and five women will be raped, depending on how many sections you skim. And whether you read faster or slower, you can't do anything to stop it.

You once read an article where the author kept referring to what happened to her (you could also write, "what was done to her") as "my rape." This makes it seem like a chronic illness, which is more accurate than you'd care to admit.

Sorry girl, can we push back brunch? My rape is acting up again this morning.

Ugh, I so feel you. A couple weeks ago my rape woke me up in the middle of the night and I couldn't get back to sleep! Thought I was feeling better but keeps happening 2-3 times a month!!! So annoying!! Hope they find a cure soon xoxox

Asking for Forgiveness, or
How to Embrace the Victim Label to Avoid Alienating People

Start by apologizing for your sort-of-rape. Apologize first for co-opting the term. Appease those who are going to be angry that you might be claiming to be part of something you're not actually part of because it's often easier than having to clarify the situation when you admit to being "assaulted" or "not really raped." Explain you've learned you can't just dangle a term like "sort-of-raped" out there and expect people not to ask you what happened. That's how you ended up telling the wrong version of your story on a crowded six train during rush hour a few years ago, because your friend just wouldn't take "sexually assaulted" for an answer. You're still worried that you implied that you were all-the-way-raped. She assumed a lot, but you could have corrected her. You should have corrected her. Instead, you just nodded because you didn't feel like getting into it on the train. So wherever she is now, she thinks the wrong version is the truth. Years later, you're still sick with worry that it counts as lying. It probably does. But everyone on the train was listening. So now everyone on the train also has the wrong story. The moral is: Always be willing to relive and talk about your rape in great detail when someone else brings it up, but never *ever* bring it up yourself.

Looks like you're due for another apology, because here you are, talking about it, ruining everyone else's good time. *Triggering people.* You're being selfish. You'll need to act fast. Explain that you know it's not only a real downer but has also been done to death. Empathize with everyone who is just so tired of hearing about rape. Be sure to throw in a few lines about how you know that all men aren't rapists, and link to a few anti-rape causes and organizations led by men so that you don't risk alienating half your audience. Throw in that quote from a male celebrity about people with power needing to stand up for people without power. For some reason, you find that usually works. Probably because you've reminded men that they have power. Who said that, again, and can you find more like it? You really can't afford to alienate the male feminists. They're a very sensitive group. They don't like feeling picked on. Appease them, right out of the gate.

While you're reading this, between two and five women will be raped, depending on how many sections you skim. And whether you read faster or slower, you can't do anything to stop it.

Next, acknowledge the inconvenience of this kind of story, the excessive heavy-handedness, the accompanying afterthoughts of guilt and depression. Apologize again for the potential triggers. Insist that you wouldn't bring it up if it weren't so important, if you didn't really need to talk about it. Thank them for doing you the honor and favor of listening to "your truth."

You know what? No, don't start with an apology. You're forgetting what the professional victim said. *If you were raped, it was not your fault.* Start with what happened itself. That's a good hook. That'll get page views. Besides, if you don't get to the good stuff until halfway down the page, people will either have already stopped reading or will be disappointed that your story didn't have enough pay-off for the time they put into it.

If You're Skimming to Get to the Rape Part, Here It Is

Start with getting ready. Start with how excited you were for your first dance. Talk about how you applied makeup with shaky hands, when it was still sold in tubes with scents like "Blooming Blueberry" or "Gorgeous Grape." Explain how you didn't know how to put on lip liner, so you settled for a light pink lip gloss from Clinique. How you straightened your blond hair until your split ends crackled between the bronze-colored clamps. And don't forget to describe the shirt. Light pink, slightly sheer, reading in gold glitter: *Blondes Have More Fun.* Say how cool you felt wearing the shirt, because it was from the store that everyone else shopped at but that you always felt you were too fat and too weird to even walk into. But now you're wearing the shirt, and you kind of like that it's advertising something. Your mother doesn't approve. Your father doesn't say anything.

Stop. You can't say that you liked the shirt and the makeup or imply that they made you feel like you were an adult. That, for sure, can and will be used against you. And to some men that would mean you were asking for it. Try again.

Start with the church. Establish the setting. But be aware that people may think this is an attack on God and religion, and that people will get defensive when they think their beliefs are being attacked. They will remind you that God didn't do this, just like guns themselves aren't *really* the things killing people. Someone broke God's law by doing this to you, just like school shooters take advantage of responsible gun owners. Mental illness, poor upbringing, absent parents, rejection—especially rejection— are responsible for these unfortunate choices. Not the church. You need to make that clear. Besides, it's confusing. People will think you mean a priest did it, that you were molested behind a confessional curtain or in the vestibule after communion, which is what people usually assume happened (like that day on the six train). But that's not what happened, and frankly what did happen is not as exciting. You feel a need to clear up the assumptions of others as if they, too, are your fault.

Look, this isn't going well. You've already told several backhanded and poorly delivered rape jokes, which is going to set off arguments over whether you, or other, better, all-the-way victims, have a right to joke about rape, even if you're employing dark humor. You've also brought God into it. You've admitted to lying, or at the very least not telling the whole truth. You've said you were wearing, well, kind of an inappropriate shirt. You've said that you liked the implications of that shirt. And you haven't even said what happened.

Start with looking him up on social media fifteen years after the fact. You find a picture of him smiling from a chrome-decked boat with a beer in one hand, the other protectively curled around a kind-looking woman. You thought she was beautiful, and for a second you allowed yourself to think that maybe he had changed, that maybe he had used the moment to become a better person, that maybe he told her, in a night filled with tears—on his end and hers—about what he did to you, about how he apologized, about how you halfway accepted his apology because there were people looking, because you were young, because you didn't really have another choice. About how you vaguely recall a note from him and his father, delivered in person on your doorstep, reading, "I am sorry for what my friends and I did." But you don't remember there being any friends. Discuss how you heard that people saw his mother sobbing in the country club lobby two days after it happened. Don't say that you liked hearing that. Talk about how you start to type up a message to the girlfriend, or maybe the fiancée, of the not-all-the-way-rapist, the barely-assault guy, and how you consume half a bottle of wine while your finger lingers over the "send" button. No. Don't start there. You sound crazy. You weren't even raped. Maybe you were just dancing and don't remember. Don't risk ruining someone's life.

Get Back to the Story

YOU'RE wearing the *Blondes Have More Fun* shirt, and you just came back from the bathroom of the church basement, where you sprayed a few more pumps of something that you can't believe was ever marketed as a "subtle scent" onto your hair and wrists. You vaguely remember that you were also wearing hairspray with flecks of gold glitter in it, and potentially even acid-wash jeans. Admitting that is just as embarrassing as talking about what happened, but it was the early 2000s and you were thirteen, so you feel like you're owed some leeway here.

The town is very conservative, and social class divides are very strong. Oddly enough, church is one of the only places in town where everyone mixes together, which feels right. You love God—you think. You have attended Christian summer camps in the mountains of North Carolina for three summers now. You enjoy praise songs, devotionals, and prayer, though you keep those sorts of things to yourself. Still, it's the kind of place, and you're at the age, where it's almost trendy to be religious. Your friends bring books with titles like *Emails from God* to sleepovers. They also use religious fasts as a way to hide their eating disorders, but that's neither here nor there. You left your old church, the Presbyterian one, because most of your friends attended the Methodist one a block away. The Methodist church also has a cooler youth pastor who orders a lot of pizza and teaches you how to tie-dye. You wonder whether you could have avoided everything if you'd just stuck with the Presbyterians.

Your friends are still putting on extra coats of their mothers' mascara, but you didn't feel like waiting on them. Tired of sitting on the sidelines, you head out to the middle of the dance floor and decide to dance by yourself. You've never been anything close to a good dancer, but you figure there's no safer place to try than God's house. You're just starting to feel confident around members of the opposite sex, but they don't seem interested in you, even with the glitter hairspray. You start to mimic some of the moves you've seen on television.

You realize suddenly that there is someone on your back, pressing, pushing into you. You don't know who it is because your neck is being held so that you can't turn it. You don't remember the exact mechanics of it, but you remember not being able to clasp your hands in prayer. Is God watching now, and, if so, should you be embarrassed? You are now in the middle of a circle of spectators as he grips you and thrusts into you and pulls at your clothes. He won't let go, and you can't get him off you. He keeps pulling you into him, harder and harder.

Slowly, you start to recognize the faces surrounding you, watching you. Some are frozen, unsure of what to do. Others gaze voyeuristically between the cracks of their fingers, pretending to shield their eyes in an attempt to appear disinterested. Some stare openly, arms folded, mouths agape, eyes wide, willing witnesses to the spectacle. There's the boy you painted benches with on your youth group trip to the orphanage. You remember how you'd flicked paint at each other that summer, writing your initials in navy blue on the seat of the bench. There's the boy who goes to your school, who has seen everything and will recount the events of tonight to everyone. Finally, there's the boy on your back, whose face you can't see but whose breath you can feel; unrelenting, hot, sticky. When you wanted to be the center of attention, this wasn't exactly what you had in mind.

Before your vision starts to blur again, you spot in the corner, withdrawn from the circle, the boy you like, the one you'd tried to look so nice for. You see that sweet and silent boy nobody ever pays much attention to, aside from you, and remember how you would always partner together for scavenger hunts in the church parking lot, how you dipped your fingers into the same bucket of green dye, gripping t-shirts bundled with rubber bands. Your hands had been stained a sickening shade for days afterward, but you'd liked looking at them because they reminded you of him.

But now he is barely looking at you from his spot in the corner. He takes off his glasses, and if things were slower you might have seen that they were fogging up. But the corner is far away from where you are, and now you've once again lost focus. You have tears in your eyes that you can't wipe away, as he is still holding your hands behind your back.

The faith is continually whisked out of you as, blinded, you twist around the room once more. You realize you've been fighting back all this time, attempting to extract yourself. You become conscious of the fact that you're kicking, screaming, beating his sides and head with a ferociousness that seems to have been building for years. Everyone is still watching, except for your friends, who are still primping in the bathroom. In your last moments as a believer, you beg God to show you some of the mercy that has made Him so famous. Finally, you land a bite on the boy's arm that loosens his grip. You leave every part of the life you once felt so certain of inside that now impenetrable circle.

An irrelevant and unknowable number of minutes later, you are sitting on the faded yellow steps just outside the basement. You can still hear the thump of the music and the laughter of your friends, a few of whom have taken rotating minute-long shifts to come check on you. Eventually, your youth pastor comes outside. He doesn't sit on the steps with you. He says one sentence: "If I didn't see it, it didn't happen." Then he walks away.

Pretend you're being interviewed for a television show.

Host: Are you glad it happened?
You: What?
Host: I mean, in the sense that if it hadn't happened, you might still be really religious and conservative, potentially bigoted, maybe a denier of feminism. Do you think you could have supported the women's rights movement fully without a tragedy to back up your narrative?
You: What?

Host: Would it be fair to say that being assaulted made you into the woman you are today?

You: I don't know.

Host: You weren't even fully raped, you know. Nothing that bad even happened. It could have been a lot worse. You should be grateful.

You: I am.

After

You start to think that after you tell your story, you will be a victim first and foremost. Everything you do will be seen by others as having been accomplished through the lens of a survivor. Your successes will be qualified, your failures undeservingly forgiven.

You find support in the strangest places, including other formerly religious people. Many of them were abused by members of their religious communities, or sometimes even the leaders of those communities. They talk about what happened to them—joke about it, even—frequently enough for you to tell them about your own experiences. They get that it wasn't just your supposed "dignity" or "agency," or whatever buzzwords you're supposed to use, that was lost—it was the security of your religious beliefs and community. Like you, nobody ever believed them either. They were told they were liars, troublemakers, people who had a problem with God and wanted to ruin it for everybody else. Because of these new friends, you finally end up addressing the situation. You watch as they confront their abusers, form support organizations, and try to stop it from happening to their own children, who of course they are no longer allowed to see. You talk each other down on bad nights; you forgive their random, angry outbursts, and they forgive yours. You realize it's "very wrong" to sit around telling jokes about your sexual assault, but you always feel better afterward, and they do too. It's a lot better than "processing your feelings" or making a collage about how you felt, or having a conversation with your inner child in the form of a stress ball, or making a "peace candle" and "lighting it to let the fear burn." It's a lot more effective, too. You're allowed to laugh at a joke, whereas if you laugh at the "peace candle" you'll probably be asked to leave. That's why you never went to therapy.

But have you thought about the consequences of speaking out?

Listen. Don't write it at all. It's really safer not to write it at all. Someone could sue you, or worse label you as the girl who's using her so-called rape that wasn't even a rape to have something to write about. You can have the most heartbreaking story in the world, but good subject matter doesn't automatically make you a good writer. Besides, rape stories are kind of passé, like addiction, parenting, or abuse memoirs. Especially, as the statistics show, everywhere somebody's got a story they're just dying to sell to a publisher. You imagine how that conversation would go: So what makes your rape different? Can you give us an Elizabeth Smart-esque narrative? Were you gang-raped daily over the course of ten years? Were you raped with an object? By members of a popular fraternity or a prominent member of a political party or religious organization? Was your rape filmed and distributed without your knowledge? That's the kind of rape we're looking for. Give us something new! And we need it to have a happy ending. We don't want young girls reading this and thinking a rape is the kind of thing you can't get over. Give us a message of empowerment!

Just move on. Don't send the message, don't ask your family what happened to the note, and for God's sake don't attach your name to this. Think of the potential employers. What happened to you may not be your fault, but how you choose to handle it is. Is this really the kind of thing you want your friends and family to be reading? Nobody can be honest about a rape piece anyway. What are they gonna say? "I hated the rape piece. I couldn't relate to it, and it was too depressing." You'll never know if people think you're a good writer or just feel sorry for you. And it's a label that's going to follow you forever if you make something like this public. *Your name: Raped.* What is this going to do to your dating life? This is the sort of thing that could be a real deal breaker to people. Think about that. When writing about your rape, be sure to consider the feelings of others. Think about whether you too are ready to become a professional victim.

You decide not to write the rape piece.

lists

Three Lists

MARYA HORNBACHER

List One: Of Theorems and Proof

1. Theorem One

What we are is a shell, the exoskeleton of space, spirals and chambers in which nothing lives.

2. Theorem Two

What we are: is the logarithmic spiral of the shell (ϕ, or 1.6180339887 . . . &c.): an irrational number. Extant only in zero-dimensional space.

3. A Problematic Fact

The irrational spiral of shell, extant only in theory, still accounts for the actual echo a child hears, holding the shell to her ear, of an ocean roaring in the farthest chamber, hidden from sight by the shell's spiral.

4. Which Can Be Understood As

illusion, of course: the whorl of the child's ear, and the blood in the ear, and the beat of the blood in the ear echo into the spiral, travel through

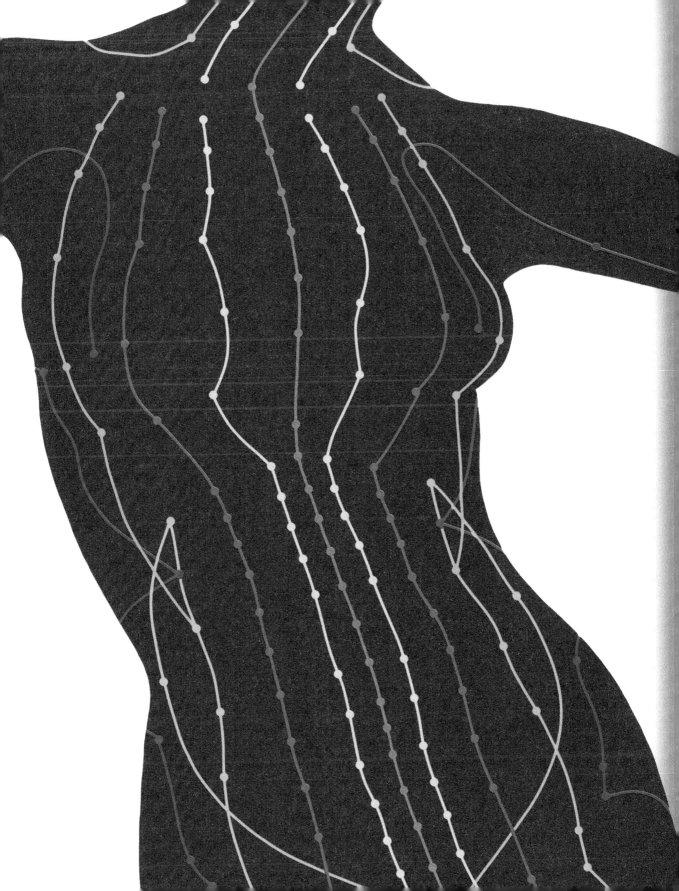

the shell's chambers into the farthest chamber and then bounce backward through the shell into the skull.

5. The Equation

The growth pattern of each subsequent chamber is phi times the size of the previous. I am speaking of the shell.

6. Theorem Three

What we are is the ear, and the number of chambers that make up the ear, the echoing chambers, the hollows of which we mostly consist.

7. An Alternative Theory

What we are is the child, growing in spirals, each empty space phi times the size of the previous, such that our empty chambers go on forever, such that if you put your ear to us you'll hear the roar of our ache and our echo, ad infinitum.

8. What There Is on the California Shore

A child in a red sweater. Kneeling in the water. Head bent to the side to listen to the shell. Also cypress, boughs heavy with hanging moss. Black pines and green pines, eucalyptus and the scent of eucalyptus and whoever held the camera and took the picture of the child listening intently to the sound of empty space.

9. The Golden Ratio

What we call beauty: the nautilus shell, the fern as it unfurls, a certain arrangement of bones, the spun helix of DNA. That which is in perfect proportion should be, by all reason, transcendent: a transcendent number, indivisible and endless, like pi.

But the spun strands of which we are made and the spaces of which we consist and the echo and the ache are illusion,

10. Proof

which is to say earthbound, kneeling in the water on the shore, consisting of salt water, and the sound of the blood in our ears, the sound of an ocean that roars deep in us where we do not exist.

List Two: Of What Lies in the Distance

1. How We Got There

We rode in the back of Nate's blue truck, passing a bottle of some cheap shit. Our skeletons danced like marionettes as we rattled over the road.

2. What We Wore

Those fake woven Mexican ponchos, cheap at the head shops. In the front pockets, we carried bags of decent Northern California pot, and pipes.

3. How Old We Were

We were fifteen. Nate was seventeen, so he had the truck.

4. The Route

We took the coast road, Highway 1. It ran north and slightly west, through the scattered hill towns that smelled of wood smoke, cedar, sweet rot. I hitched a ride to the main road as the sun slid down behind the eucalyptus trees. The boys tore up around the bend, and I swung in.

5. What It Is

A shallow, rocky inlet of the Pacific Ocean, five miles across, bordered on the north by Bodega Head and flowing south into Tomales Bay. It lies pressed up close against the San Andreas Fault like one body pressed against the length of another, both rippling with seismic shocks.

6. What We Did As We Approached

We lifted our faces to smell for salt, our hair all tangled up with wind. We took slugs off the bottle and howled and laughed. The eucalyptus burned the nostrils and lungs, and so did the sweet cloves we smoked.

7. What This Was Before

This was before he kissed me behind the bloodflower. This was before I knew there was a plant called bloodflower, and one called cathedral bells, before I knew prayer plant, before I could incant them, whispering names as I walked through the dunes, before I walked through the dunes later, alone. Flora that thrive here include purple iceplant, yellow desert daisy, iris, agave, water lily, bleeding heart, flame azalea, rosary vine. This was before the whiskey kiss behind the bloodflower and high sage. This was before the kiss sealed my mouth with death. The boy died. I tasted whiskey when I heard he had. The taste of whiskey on a child's fevered breath.

8. What Happens There

The road peters out, turns to sand. Now, in the darkness, you can hear it, the heave and crash of the ocean, taste salt spray on your lips. There's little light, just the truck's high beams scanning fences, running over the pampas grass's white plumes. We rattle to a stop, jump out, run barefoot into the dunes. Hissing sand grass rushes against our legs; we stumble on the shifting earth. We build a fire of driftwood scraps, sit with our legs drawn up against our chests. Sit staring into the fire, passing the bottle and the pipe. The black night pours itself into the well of itself.

9. What There Is in the Distance

The brackish marsh.
 The wet meadow.
 The freshwater marsh.
 The tidal lagoon, and the creatures therein.
 Sandpiper, egret, blue heron, bobcat, the red-legged frog.
 In the sleeping bay, black as oil, the seal, sea lion, and whale.

10. How He Did It

A length of rope.

11. Who Found Him

His brother, after school.

12. What His Mother Did at the Funeral

An interpretive dance. She'd gone crazy years before and no longer spoke. The congregation looked away as she danced up and down the aisles, mimed giving birth, mimed nursing him, rocking him, mimed him hanging from the rope. She held her hands to her throat till she turned purple, tongue lolling from her mouth. Someone had to pry her hands away. Then she sat down.

13. What I Did after the Funeral

Drove north and slightly west through the hill towns where the boys had lived. The sun slid down behind the trees. The smell of eucalyptus burned my nose and lungs. I drove fast, my hair all tangled up with wind. I got out of the car, took off my shoes, walked barefoot through the dunes. The sand was cold and smooth. My lips tasted of whiskey, salt spray, sweet cloves.

I walked down to the water. What there is by the water: tide pool, rope of kelp, spume, foam. I walked until I could no longer feel his seeking mouth, his hunger, his unanswerable ache.

List Three: Of Seven Dreams

1.

Somewhere outside a woman is laughing. Last night I dreamed I spoke Spanish. I don't. I dreamed I knew the words *tumelo domo*. I dreamed they meant *little pig*. They do not. I looked them up. They mean *burial mound*. They mean *grave*.

2.

This is the dream of the centrifuge, or fast dancing. The question is raised: whether to address the theory or, instead, the application of spinning and distribution of dense things equally over a given object or space. Even in the dream, this makes no sense.

3.

This is the dream where I'm sick with betrayal. No one betrays me. I have betrayed. I wake reeling, holding my face. I know the face in the dream. Always, I know the face I betray. They cry out when they discover what I've done.

4.

If I sit long enough in the darkening room, my body disappears piece by piece. My hands are last to be erased. Then, invisible, I go to sleep, and this is when I dream of erasure, of being a thing that, in darkness, is dispersed.

Generally this is when the lover in bed shakes me awake because I am screaming. The lover always says, *Shh. It's all right, it's all right.*

It isn't, of course. It is not all right.

5.

This is the dream where I am shot. Three times. Three times, I die. There is a moment after dying, it turns out, where you think, *Is this it? Am I dead?* You look around, try to move your arms and legs. But you are only mind, only a searchlight of eyes.

6.

What's known: the mathematics of breathing. You told me this once. You lay sleeping. Eyes closed, you said, *It's simple; each heartbeat is assigned a number of breaths. This number is four.* You held your hands this far apart, to show the approximate measure of breath.

I said, *You're sleeping.* But you insisted you were not, and perhaps you were not. Perhaps my breath is measured in the space between your hands.

7.

In this dream, I am old. It is the dream where I reach up and touch my face. When I take my hands away, they are covered with papery skin, brittle-boned. In the dream, I push through a crowd, search for a mirror, see myself: my hair crow-black and straight as straw. I hold my face in my hands. The skin wrinkles, sags over my fingers. My cheeks become jowls, the skin under my eyes droops until the whites gleam. My mouth comes off, lips curling away from the gums. I am holding my face to my skull.

Vaguely, I know that you are somewhere nearby, maybe somewhere in the crowd, and I know that this is a dream about you.

12 Letters to the CosmoMutt

LIZ N. CLIFT

1.

Dear Laika: When you were a pup, and living on the streets in Moscow, did you howl at the moon and the stars?

2.

Dear Laika: Did you have a person? Someone who secreted you scraps? I like to imagine a small child tossing you crusts of bread and the grisly parts of whatever meat their mother may have had. I like to imagine you thumping your tail as they approached, but eyes watchful, ready to run.

3.

Dear L: I always call my own dog pup, even though she is years beyond puppyhood.

It might be a way for me to pretend that I can prolong her life. That I haven't already had more days with her than I have left with her.

4.

L: I first read about you in elementary school. The book didn't mention you died up there, so I imagined you still circling the earth. Forty years and counting. Looking down on us. Lonely for humans and fresh kibble.

5.

You only made it to your fourth orbit around the sun. The ship was too hot—more than a hundred degrees, and humid. I imagine you trying to press your belly to the floor, and not being able to because of that whole weightlessness thing.

I imagine you shaking, the way my pup does when fireworks explode.

Maybe you thought about Yazdovsky's children playing with you. Maybe you yearned for the pack of humans who'd comforted you after centrifuge tests.

6.

I know a little something about broken trust.

I know a little something about wishing the people who broke your trust would comfort you, the confusion and fear that follow.

7.

Laika: You didn't blame yourself, did you?

8.

Here's the thing, Laika. People aren't like dogs. We do shitty things, and then we blame those we hurt for being hurt. Maybe we say it's for science. Maybe we say it's for the person's own good.

It's our way of lying to ourselves, because we can't let ourselves imagine that maybe we're really monsters.

Even the scientists who sent you into space said, decades later, they didn't think it was worth it.

They never planned to bring you home.

9.

Here's the thing, Laika. Most people believe the shitty things that are said and done to them are their fault.

Take, for instance, the days after I was raped. I spent hours looking up the definition of rape (was it *really* rape?). I spent day after day considering what I should have said or done differently earlier in the night. I spent months believing that my response, which was to go slack, was my fault.

I panicked whenever I saw a white pickup like his.

I panicked whenever something felt out of my control.

Sometimes, looking back, it seems like I spent the next two years either crying or being numb.

Because even when I said the right things: *It's not my fault. He did this to me. The person who is raped is not to blame—someone else made the decision to commit an act of violence.* I didn't really believe it.

I didn't really believe it, because the world told me otherwise.

10.

It was not your fault.

You were not a bad dog.

11.

Dear L: People still love you. There are songs written about you. There's a comic, in which you are a hero—so much so that the man who made the comic had to write an alternate ending because no one liked the one where you died.

12.

Maybe part of the reason so many people want you to come home is because we want to believe, in the face of all evidence to the contrary, that the world is just.

13 Things Your Mail Carrier Won't Tell You

—Headline from February 2011—

SARAH LAYDEN

1. It's not about the dogs, but control. That you should learn to tame the untamed. That to let your pit bull ride shotgun is one step removed from handing over the keys. Barking, fine. That can be controlled. As can you.

2. If you invited me inside to meet your new baby, I would come in. I would tread lightly on the floorboards; I would ignore your unkempt hair and rustblood birthscent, and that your scraggly chicken infant in his carrier has just shat himself. I would murmur, *Beautiful, lovely, beautiful.*

3. Only once have I been invited inside a house on my route. Twenty years have passed, and I still cannot talk about it.

4. Some children toddle down the sidewalk, impatient parents dragging them by one arm. These adults glower, eye-circled and minimally attentive, unwilling to accept the importance of even the junk mail. The life-saving products and offers such mail contains.

5. What you worried I saw through the parted curtains: I saw. I will not tell unless I need to. Who can say what need is?

6. Upon viewing tattoos on forearms and calves, I used to think, *Wastrel, trash.* Now I see cave pictures made flesh. Absence and sorrow.

7. A decrease in Book-of-the-Month selections lightens my load and weighs on my mind. I adored *The Brothers Karamazov.* I delighted in Nabokov. Daily I show my age, a trouble that does not cease.

8. The boots are comfortable enough to sleep in.

9. I make up stories about the shut-ins. Who among us has not wondered if the rumors about Dead Harry are true? That his plumbing broke and his knees didn't work so the bathtub became a toilet. I saw the man from the realtor's cleaning service, retching on the lawn.

10. All the gossips are lonely. Deep, deeper, deeply. A loneliness of the soul.

11. Planting flower beds here or there wouldn't kill you. Nothing too showy. This is my backdrop, my office.

12. It was not the war, not overseas, not in uniform. But I was part of two battles. They did not tell us where we were. We met the man we were instructed to terminate. We shook his hand; we smiled into his face. We gave him a two-hour head start. This was practice, they said. Brave faces, they said. Warrior hearts, we chanted.

13. When I put the third letter in your box upside down:

       this is my way of saying

       I love you.

poetry

If You and I Said *Fuck It,* and Bought the Ranch in Montana

H. K. HUMMEL

I'd have hands that could set bone
or arc a two-bit axe.

I'd study how gravity pulls sugar through apple,
what it means to straighten a river,

to keep a clutch of cedar waxwings
coming back.

You'd have a mountain ridge rain-shadow,
a distortion in your voice like trout under creek water;

your hands would untangle fishing nets,
or our child's wet hair. You'd listen to how stillness

breaks in front of an avalanche,
the way elk disappear into serviceberry,

what silences surround an instarring gypsy moth.

Yesterday's Bestiary for Tomorrow

H. K. HUMMEL

The ivory-billed woodpecker knockers us in the swampy bottomlands with an axiom on survival. We memorize its red mohawk and high-pitched toot, *kent, kent, kent,* then search the bald cypress and tupelo as if looking for Aristotle's half-soul. If desire can be prayer, we might say *let us be here together.* How we listen, these little epochs.

*

A school of akule columns into the hosanna of us, a trembling knot of this every only now. A shirring big-eyed wonder-mess of unified goldshine. Boundaries redefined mid-whirl. Now a globe, an atoll, a flying buttress. Togetherness manifest, togetherness solidified, togetherness as an act of defiance. As trust of other.

*

When it comes, it is the sensation of peering through a View-Master: sage scrub hills of San Clemente Island invaded by sea. Kodachrome tints circa 1979: aqua and goldenrod. I scissor-kicked beyond the 3-D loom of the cliffs, listening to the water sigh against sandstone. My brother, face down beside me, rasped through a snorkel. He popped up blinking, coughing. A manta ray bigger than us: a diamond of night sky fluttering below. Our feet touched nothingness. We weren't afraid.

Alien Invasions at the Evans Salvage Grocery

M. D. MYERS

You look past dents in the cans.
      Bruised fruit-flesh—that's fine.
            But boxes, you have to inspect the seams.

At fifteen, I pretend sci-fi—

      [the food comes to us from far away.
      has had a rough journey from earth to this
      boiling rock. we've been marooned. maybe
      we were criminals, who knows, who cares anymore.
      survive. don't get eaten.
            sometimes we are invaded]

At fifteen, I bring home grain beetles

for the second time. Secret breach. They sing in the cupboard
      in the box in the rice. After three days I wake
         to my sister's reproach—
         check the seams.

This all has to go.
[they're everywhere cry the abandoned colonists]

She fights for a week against their gleaming
    incursion. Seed-bodies, tiny mouths, wanton
        & hungry in the cabinets. Then gassed.
            Popped like seeds, small implosions of air.

        [i am still scraping along on that planet   rationing
        the good oxygen   failing to check the frontiers for risk]

Last night you were fighting
    with bottles again—I drove you
        by the house my mother was made
            to give back, where I pretend

the invaders I unknowingly smuggled as a child
    are germinating in the dark kitchen.
        [they have been waiting for years   growing in size and
          hunger]
           We know a thing or two about family

setting fire to the carpet beneath
    our homely feet. The new owners keep
        the grass short, don't collect trash
            like curios. But they saved the swing

my grandfather hung, & its tree was still strong.
    Swinging with you under the bottle-
        colored moon, we listened together
            [different invasions
    familiar alien
        glittering seed-song—
            high & old & hungry]

[If you said *kitchen* and meant *harden* and then if you walked out back and forgot]

KALLIE FALANDAYS

If you said *kitchen* and meant *harden* and then if you walked out back
   and forgot to look at the sky   what if all of the boys you kissed
   were just hungry?
What if you fed them skin and so, when they said *tree,* you heard *hollow.*
What if you were hungry and so you walked around with your hands out
saying *children, bricks, light bulbs*:
something to remember, to carry, to leave behind.
And then, when all of the strangers on the bus turned to you at once
and said things like *postage, letterbox, faucet.*
If everyone knew what you meant, you wouldn't have to say
your lips are fluttering porcelain, or *even my eyes burn like ten thousand fire*
   escapes breaking.
If, when you turned to everyone and said *puree, timber, rustling,*
they all looked to the west and nodded their heads.

Orbit

HELENA CHUNG

after Yayoi Kusama

I'm a coward / could not say what scares / me most I want to live

in the moon hide / in her coarse craters (close / the eyes)

we would punch the air from inside her / dirty sedan

our mouths round / and wet our shoes / pointed

glistening with field / dew from a swath / we'd just disturbed

if I asked / for a spaceship my mother / would point

to her / belly as if to say my oh my / you've already forgotten

the man had never squashed / fruit for plum wine / his hands stained

pink for what / seemed like forever after / I stuffed

the white fabric I remembered / the beauty that launched one thousand

harbors into solitude / but what of a woman who can tear

only one dinghy away from a boat / house in summer

the lake thick / with yellow tail the moon / clipped to a crescent

no I thrive / in small spaces the backseats / of black cars hurtling down

95 the moon pressing her face / against the glass the moon

turning the dials slowly.

In Defense of Being the Other Woman

SARAH DALTON

There are only a few things I'm not proud of: knuckle tattoos and the nights you smelled like matrimony. In my bed, you slept in sweat, and I paced in the kitchen, practicing long division. If you weren't the spit in my shower drain or the crack in stucco that once fit my finger, I could have loved you until you were anxious. But you're still a Sagittarius, and I'm still in Michigan mourning over dead skin, falling in love with the sound of my own voice making excuses.

Poem Where I Almost Hit a Coyote

ARIANE SANDFORD

I almost hit a coyote on the drive back from the hospital
where my friend who'd just had a baby held the tiny thing near her
    mouth while it
made whimpering animal noises
her first baby since the last strangled itself in utero

I almost hit a coyote, I thought as I almost hit a coyote, jammed my right
    foot on the
brakes, outline of its ears limned against darkening sky and the haze of
    airport lights

I almost hit a coyote on October 23, 2015, while the sky was darkening
    and the cells of
my friend's dead baby swam in her bloodstream still, finding permanent
    residence in
her lungs, thyroid, muscle, liver, heart, kidneys, skin, and brain

I almost hit a coyote who was probably heading home for the night,
    maybe after

finishing a delicate meal of mouse and blood soup, and if I had a home
    in the body I

would hope to do better than the brain

that mouse-gray noodle farm we dissected once for biology class in high
    school

where the teacher in her lonely British accent told us that it was the brain
    of an

alcoholic female

and the brain just lay there, flat and neat and quiet

though I don't remember how she knew that

I almost hit a coyote on the way back from the hospital, while my friend
    pretended to

love her living baby as much as her dead one, and the ghost cells of her
    dead baby

whispered in her ear that it was part coyote, and moon, tall northern
    pine, and trout

breaching lake water at dawn.

Calling Her Names

STEVIE EDWARDS

Call her crick in my neck I thought the chiropractor fixed
wolf that picked me up by the scruff to keep
                              as a play thing
a play, I can't figure out my lines, where the audience sits
                    a plush purple chair in my past with cigarette burns
where my death sits   where she screams out
        at a man throwing me around a living room
dance party   poor swing dancer   where she screams me out
        of a cab   the man caught pouring
his martini into mine   again and again   Beauty
Bar   Chicago   Call her the love
        that eats me for breakfast   Call her the love
that asks for my hand   in tornado
        and barfly   in stomp out the room until
it's time to be a better song   call her chaos-
lover   call her   burns the whole damn house down
        after eviction   call her house   call her
changed phone number   call her   I can't
        pull scrap metal from a field   and build a getaway

car   can't play fiddle with toxic strings   can't play
dead anymore   call her disaster   porn
call her *I'm too fucking tired to look anymore*   call her and say
it's okay you're okay it's okay   call her my name

After Party

STEVIE EDWARDS

After the party there is the after party and after the after
party there is the after after party. Trash

dance. Flash romance with a handsome
bar tab. Radiant night held in a gulp of blank

goodbye. Goodbye moon, my name is
wonder cunt. You can't pull

the blood out of me with your bright stare
tonight. Goodbye romance,

my game is Hearts. I am always two-suited
and too slick for you. I take the spade

queen out for brunch. Bitch loves hollandaise
like I hate holidays. It's not that kind

of party. No eggnog, no glittering evergreens—
beer and bacardi, a room whirling

bodies around its bloated belly. Goodbye
dance floor, I am warm and radial. Redial

the number of a man who called me
cunt and meant *abscess* or *absence*. Absinthe

makes the heart grow glow. I can go out
into the street and piss my name if I want to,

cry if I want to, die if I want to, kiss
my bare knees if I want to. But it's not my party.

Nothing stops when I wander. Bachata
booming through the snowy lawn. No voice

of God or concerned confidant asking
what tide pulls me out out and away

from the fun of neck musk sugar legs
galore. When I kneel down in the driveway

cooing, *It was never your fault*—to a girl
in a Holiday Inn a decade ago drowned

in the opposite of yes, that dread water, I am
more scabbed than taffeta dress. I slide into a glass

of whatever is left inside. Lazy spells for riddance:
Do I look pretty in this drink? Goodbye wonder,

my game is darts. I barely hit the board.
Goodbye handsome pulling a coat over me.

Flash into the after the after after party
cab. Into I am a sore site for worship and need

hollandaise and aspirin. Into don't call me
until this goodbye sky fades back into a woman.

lawn mower one

BETSY JOHNSON-MILLER

the lawn mower is a strange place to have an argument
with my father   it's loud   he's deaf   and
dead   my father the coroner loved to mow

like he was performing an autopsy   lines   straight
as the number 4   pencils he used extra hard always
sharp

every time I mow   I Van Gogh   green curlicues
let's call this what it is   moody work

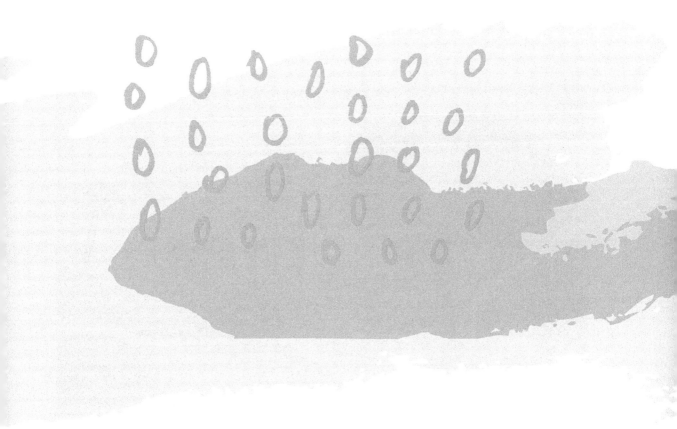

fiction

OUR TREE WAS A SOURCE OF COMFORT.

CHILDREN CLIMBED OUTSTRETCHED LIMBS.

LESS ADVENTUROUS ADULTS GRABBED BRANCHES WITH HOOKS ON LONG BAMBOO POLES. EACH REACHED FOR CLUSTERS OF UNRIPENED FRUIT.

BRANCHES SHOOK AS CLUSTERS QUIVERED AND FELL CRASHING TO THE DIRT. KIDS TOO SMALL TO CLIMB DODGED THE PLUMMETING FRUIT.

STOP RUNNIN' AROUND!

HELP PICK THE MANGOES OFF THE GROUND!

SMILES AND LAUGHTER FILLED THE WARM AIR.

OVERFLOWING SACKS SPRAWLED ON CLEAN LINOLEUM FLOORS AS WE WASHED, PEELED, AND SLICED. JARS AND THEIR BLUE LIDS WAITED, STILL HOT FROM THE STOVE.

PINK VINEGAR POURED INTO MANGO FILLED BOTTLES. STAINED FINGERS PRESSED DOWN FIRM SLICES.

EVERY YEAR WE WOULD BRING OUR PICKLE MANGO TO THE MAY DAY FESTIVAL.

OUR TABLE SAT NEXT TO THE ROYAL COURT'S STAGES.

EACH STAGE AN ISLAND DECORATED IN ITS ROYAL COLOR.

UPON THESE SAT PRINCESSES ADORNED IN LEHUA, MOKIHANA, AND HINAHINA BLOSSOMS.

THEIR ESCORTS DRIPPING IN MAILE LEIS, FRAGRANT GREEN VINES BRUSHING AGAINST KNEES.

WITH PEOPLE LINING UP TO BUY OUR FAMILY SPECIALTY, WE PRIDED OURSELVES ON SELLING ALL OF OUR PICKLES EVERY YEAR.

BUT THERE WOULD BE NO MAY DAY PICKLES THIS YEAR.

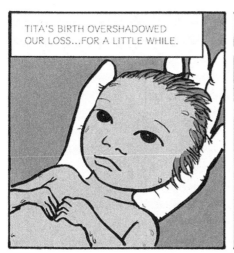

TITA'S BIRTH OVERSHADOWED OUR LOSS...FOR A LITTLE WHILE.

WHEN SHE CAME INTO THE WORLD SHE WAS A BUNDLE OF STILLNESS.

SHE DID NOT GREET US WITH A HEARTY CRY TO PROVE HER EXISTENCE.

WHEN WE TOOK HER HOME FROM THE HOSPITAL, THE NURSES ADMIRED HER SILENCE.

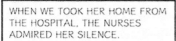

WHAT A GOOD BABY!

SHE NEVER SMILED. SHE NEVER EVEN CRIED. HER PINK LIMBS NEVER FLAILING TO BE COMFORTED.

WE COULD NOT BRING OURSELVES TO ADMIT, TO PIERCE THE AIR WITH A SUGGESTION OF ABNORMALITY.

WE WANTED A GIGGLE, A GURGLE, A GOO...

WE SEARCHED FOR ANY SIGN OF THE ORDINARY.

IN HER CRIB, SHE WOULD STARE BEYOND HER TROPICAL FISH MOBILE, OUT THE LOUVERED WINDOW AT SOME IMPERCEPTIBLE POINT.

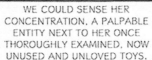

WE COULD SENSE HER CONCENTRATION, A PALPABLE ENTITY NEXT TO HER ONCE THOROUGHLY EXAMINED, NOW UNUSED AND UNLOVED TOYS.

WE WONDERED. AND WE WAITED.

WE HOPED SHE WOULD RESPOND TO OUR ATTEMPTS AT CAJOLERY, DISTORTED FACES, HIGH-PITCHED NOISES.

LOOK AT DADDY!

SMILE AT MOMMY!

WHO'S GOT CUTE LITTLE FEET? AUNTIE'S GONNA EAT THOSE CUTE LITTLE FEET!

ALL OF US COMPETING WITH AN ALIEN INDIFFERENCE.

SHE DID NOT ACKNOWLEDGE PLEASURE OR DISCOMFORT.

SHE ACCEPTED OUR MINISTRATIONS WITHOUT COMPLIANCE OR COMPLAINT

NO KICKING LEGS OR WANDERING HANDS.

NO CRIES.

WE NEVER KNEW WHEN SHE WAS HUNGRY. WHEN SHE DID EAT, HER TONGUE METHODICALLY EXPLORED THE BOTTLE'S NIPPLE.

HER HANDS MOVED SLOWLY OVER THE SMOOTH SIDES.

WE WANTED HER TO TAKE PLEASURE IN PHENOMENA, BUT SHE GAVE US NOTHING.

FINALLY, WE TOOK HER OUT INTO THE WORLD.

ANXIOUSLY WE AWAITED SOME SIGNAL, A MESSAGE OF APPRECIATION FROM HER

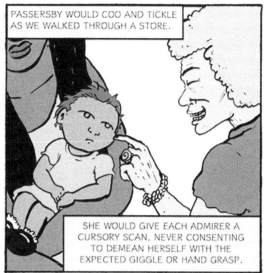

PASSERSBY WOULD COO AND TICKLE AS WE WALKED THROUGH A STORE.

SHE WOULD GIVE EACH ADMIRER A CURSORY SCAN, NEVER CONSENTING TO DEMEAN HERSELF WITH THE EXPECTED GIGGLE OR HAND GRASP.

WHAT A CUTE BABY!

HOW MANY MONTHS?

IS SHE ALRIGHT?

WE HOPED.

WE BEGAN TO AVOID HER.

WE DIDN'T WANT TO HOLD HER.

WE WOULD WALK PAST HER ROOM, DENYING HER EXISTENCE.

NO PEEK-A-BOO, NO SWEET LULLABY, NO MAKE-BELIEVE.

WE WERE AFRAID.

THEN, ONE DAY...

TITA BEGAN TO WALK.

SHE PICKED HERSELF UP AND WALKED OUT OF HER ROOM.

NO WOBBLES OR FALLS.

JUST HER LITTLE LEGS WALKING AS IF IT WERE THE EASIEST THING IN THE WORLD.

SHE STRODE THROUGH THE HOUSE, INTENTLY EXAMINING EACH ITEM.

WHAT IS SHE DOING?

HER HANDS WERE NOT THE CLUMSY TOOLS OF AN INFANT, BUT SKILLFUL INSTRUMENTS.

WHAT IS SHE LOOKING FOR?

THEY DID NOT LINGER OR PAUSE.

WE THOUGHT "WHAT AN EXCEPTIONAL CHILD" AND WELCOMED HER GENIUS AS IF HER ACTIONS WERE THE RESULT OF OUR OWN MANUFACTURE.

SHE LIFTED AND REPLACED THE SUBSTANCE OF OUR LIVES SO DEFTLY.

AT LAST, SHE WALKED INTO THE KITCHEN.

SHE TURNED AROUND...

...WENT BACK TO HER ROOM...

...AND STOPPED WALKING ALTOGETHER.

HER SILENCE INFECTED OUR LIVES. STILL AFRAID TO VOICE OUR FEARS, WORDS DRIFTED THROUGH OUR MINDS.

ABBERANT.

UNNATURAL.

ODD.

WE NEEDED HER TO BE MORE THAN A CONFIRMATION OF OUR GENIUS. SO WE BEGAN TO QUESTION OUR OWN MOTIVES AS WE OBSERVED HER.

IT WAS AS IF A BUBBLE HAD FORMED AROUND HER, PUSHING OUTWARD, ENCROACHING ON OUR LIVES.

UNKNOWINGLY, WE WELCOMED ITS EMPTY EMBRACE.

IN THE NIGHT, AN AROMA FLOATED THROUGH THE HOUSE.

A Girl Is (Not) a Pirate Ship

ERIN KATE RYAN

INFATUATED WITH ITS OWN DECAY, an abandoned overpass has spilled its steel girder guts and boxed up the face built by humankind.

The overpass swans in its solitude, naked in the rain. The cats in the cracks have already moved on, and the overpass hums with frogsong.

The overpass was once a forest, was once a stockyard, was once a town. Its layers have all been wrenched up and left to drift back down. All lily pads are overturned, and there is nothing more here for a conquistador. (Aged and dusty, the overpass grieves its loamy forest floor.)

Like a boxing turtle: a girl, the human kind, enters the moment and elects a fighting stance. She has just crossed Missouri, stealing shelter from doorways and coffee cans. A persimmon tree is tucked beneath her girlish tongue, and her sugared breath feathers a foreign fog. Biographers barnacle, trailing her unwelcome boots.

The overpass has not yet seen such a thing as this.

And the overpass will brook no foreign share in its long-last solitude. A girl is not a pirate ship, and the overpass was never a sea.

The foreign girl does not hear the overpass object. Her conquering boots make hums of their own, and her pockets knock with turtle shells.

The rain has passed. A brook raps at her boots. The girl hoists the brook onto her turned swan shoulder and squares to face her biographers. She could be branded a pirate for this, but traveling light is no longer required.

"All I seek is solitude," she says. "I have crossed Kentucky to shake you off, and still you puddle at my feet."

Biographers in bishop hats elbow at one another for spots. They poise their feathered pens. And in that moment the overpass (this once-forest floor), crumbling scholar of humankind, recognizes false demure. Its quietude is numbered; its solace has been conquised. The foreign girl will plant a claim in what's not hers for sharing.

There is a story here, of a spiteful girl who crosses Illiana smelling of sugar and plants a bruised fruit tree.

Biographers bow their bishop hats in solemn preparation. They too can see their subject's cracks. Cracks will crack in time.

And so: the foreign girl, surprising only herself, concedes to perform for her biographers.

She tosses them her turtle shells—

"I harbor twenty-six hopes for humankind, and I know six ways to skin a cat. Both humans and cats have reason to fear me. Elegance, as in everything, is imperative."

She shuffles her boots and turns toward the overpass, *mise en* scene for dramatic reclusion.

But solitude is not for sharing. The once-forest floor is a pocket only for imagined leaves, and it wants no footnote in the girl's foreign song.

Cracks will crack in time.

The once-forest floor heaves in growing despair, and the imagined leaves contract around the foreign girl's feet (boots bruised from her conquising). They will translate the girl's twenty-six hopes into frogsong so that liability will be limited. A girl is not a pirate ship, and the once-forest floor is no sea, but it will hold her hostage, it will tie her to the mast, until she returns the leaves to the trees, until she prays for sleet.

"The rain has a past," the foreign girl says. "And the barometer is stuck on fair." Big hats bob, and feathered pens scratch at rigid turtle shells.

"I harbor twenty-six hopes for humankind." The words garble around the sugar-sweet tree. "Yiy yahbool pwenny-six obes. Pweddy-sis obdes."

Biographers consult: there is trouble in the translating.

"Twenty-six hopes for humankind, and twenty-four of them rely on your extinction. Cats and biographers have reason to fear me."

Bishop hats consult: but who will be left to biograph?

The pirate girl's plan is concrete. She has crossed Kendiana to plant this persimmon tree, and beneath the tree a coffee can of extinguished thoughts. There will be no cats to clamber the tree, and the brook will translate the leaves into yawns. The girl will hold her sugared tongue, and the tree will blaze into quiet.

Turtle shells titter; biographers have no capacity for quiet.

The once-forest floor cements itself; it will be no harbor for humankind, and the frogs need space to sing. The overpass will set the girl's barometer like a compass and steer her swan shoulders back from whence they came. There's no room for a girl who would set sail around the world in a coffee can, just obdes for an oar. She can fly a steel brook as her pirate ship flag, yet she cannot do it here. Here is already spoken for. The cats have already moved on.

But resolve cannot conquise defeat.

The once-forest floor has lost its fighting chance, as the girl poises her boots in the moment. This pirate girl has made a name on being one who steers her own ship, and before the biographers she will have her swan song. A plant of her boot, and a new hole in the asphalt. The once-forest floor abhors being known.

The foreign girl plants the pirated tree and tucks in the brook to ballast the roots. There is a story here, of a spiteful girl who crosses Illiana smelling of sugar and plants a bruised fruit tree. A girl who bruises oversimmons and crosses sugarplants. But the once-forest floor will not languish as a footnote, and biographers are bound to be wrong. Footnotes take up too much space, and frogs have their own solitude to sing. The rain is on their lips already.

There is a story here, of a conquistador who crosses Tenntucky and melts steel feathers into sea. She could slit a pirate's throat for less, and biographers have a fetish for gore. The foreign girl has a fetish for pirate ships, and this ship makes pweddy-sis.—

She will build a ship for her biographers here, a prison for footnotes and bobbing bishop hats. She will string high a frog-skin sail and raise the steel song mast. She will cobble cannons from turtle shells, and the knocking will keep us from sleep. (There is a danger here: Tired biographers are sloppy with detail. She could lose her sugared breath, her boots; her persimmons might melt into cherries. There is no elegance in cherries.)

The once-forest floor, reader of the human kind, can foretell the pirate ship's fate.

Biographers' barometers are stuck on fair; they can't pocket the elegance in barbarity. They cannot write the enduring despair—of an overpass, a frog, or a girl. Things brutal and quiet get lost in the translating; pliability is ever unlimited.

So the pirate girl will get her ship, will despair the once-forest floor into sea. She will hold her tongue, take shelter on lily pads, and tend to her loamy bruised tree. The conquistador will plunder another's solitude for her own, and the overpass's obdes will rot into rain.

But this pirate ship, who's been crossed by Ohsouri, who planted her story and buried her boot, cannot lay claim without the past sharing.

She'll be kept from sleep by the blazing brook song and the echoing hymn of the frogs. Her boots will harden into cement, and she too will be trespassed upon.

The overpass was once a stockyard, was once a forest, was once a girl. The biographers get it wrong in their ship, but there's no solace to be found in comparing.

Dear Nobody

AFTER TWENTY THOUSAND LEAGUES UNDER THE SEA *BY JULES VERNE*

KIRSTY LOGAN

07:00 / 01 March / lat 20 N long 40 W / temp -2°C

Strong currents from NE all day. Pressure good. Several shoals. Awake 16 hours.

Dear Nobody,

　　Last night I ventured out to hunt the squid. I swear I saw it. A glimpse of skull-sized eye, the twist and tentacle-grasp as it passed. A different squid than the one we fought, perhaps, but who can tell? Back then it was we, but now it's just me. I'm the only one left now. Me with my own deafening breath, tethered to the ship in my diving suit, floating with a gun in each hand in this depthless dark, cold to the marrow of my bones, the only hot blood for miles. I blink hard to see stars. Alone down here, I'm barely even a man anymore. But that was always the plan, wasn't it? ~~To lose our manhood, our humanity, in the hot blood of~~

23:44 / 03 March / lat 30 N long 40 W / temp -3°C

Currents calm. Out in suit to clear rudders, nothing to report. Awake 20 hours.

Dear Nobody,

Should we try again? We had such adventures. The coral reefs. The sunken wrecks. The ice shelves. We can follow the telegraph cable from coast to coast, slipping space-lost through the seas. We can rediscover Atlantis and lose it again. The sharks and the squid, our air guns loaded with glass bullets.

Remember what we read about dead men? How over time coral builds up over the graves, sealing the bodies. How the dead sleep under the waves, out of the reach of sharks and men. ~~If we tried again, we could make so much coral~~

01:40 / 10 March / lat 35 N long 40 W / temp -1°C

Currents changeable. Whales. Seals. Awake 36 hours.

Dear Nobody,

I've been reading our books, eager to hear a voice in my head that isn't my own. Books always say that a thing is like another thing. The same might be said of us. Books always make me think of you, because you seem to be a lot of things while hiding what you really are. So here are the things that we are like:

The green-glow ruins of Atlantis, the carpet of bones, the silence. We found a volcano there, just like the one that ruined it all, but still alive, exploding underwater.

The undersea forest, the tall street of seaweed that grew from the ocean floor, all the way to the surface. They grew straight and strong, and you said that when you bend one of the plants it immediately straightens itself again like nothing ever happened.

The—

Oh, this is useless.

It doesn't matter if you don't remember, Nemo. Just tell me we can try again. It could be different if you want, or it could be the same. ~~We got so good at those underwater funerals, we hid the men so holy, the coral will have grown, and the ocean is vaster than~~

23:44 / 30 April / lat 50 N long 60 W / temp -1°C

Some currents. Some pressure. Some sleep.

Dear Nobody,

When we first came to your ship, you let us believe you couldn't speak our language. You knew every word we said but let us speak because you wanted to know us, how we spoke when we thought you couldn't understand.

But now I think that you and I were the only ones who really spoke the same language. You said you were not a civilized man. You said you were finished with the world, and would not obey its laws. Your words went right to the heart of me.

You taught me so much. The proper angles of smiles and frowns. The right times to agree and disagree. How to be friendly, how to feign sleep, how to prowl the submarine undetected. How to pass among them. How to be the last suspected.

I was shocked when I found out what you were doing, the person you truly were. I don't think I ever told you that. Perhaps shock is the wrong word: It was more a recognition. Like looking in the mirror when all you've seen before is windows. The clue is in the name, you said with a smile, standing there with the man still slumped and dripping in the corner and the blood thick up to your wrists. The name: Nemo. *No-man.* One need not be a man when exempt from the petty laws and morals of men. The things we did, the blood still to come on both our wrists. ~~So many sailors with no one to miss them when we~~

00:00 / May, perhaps / temp 0°C

No change.
Dear Nobody,

I said once that your words had touched my weak point, namely my great interest in learning. But that was never my weak point. You didn't even have to find it, because my weakness was yours. Was you.

You know I'm still here. You know, so why aren't you here? You know I'd never hurt you. ~~I only want us to be together again, so we can hurt~~

00:00 / 00 / 0°C

Dear Nobody,

I don't know where or when I am. It doesn't matter. All that matters is you. The blood, the last breaths, the souls we sent to rest. It means nothing without you.

If I surface, will you find me? Will they? I fear you have told them what we did. I traverse the endless ocean alone as a man on the run. A no-man. A wanted man, no longer wanted.

Cliffs of Tojinbo

CATHY ULRICH

IF I WERE A TEMPORARY worker in Japan, I would take one of my days off and go to Tojinbo to gaze out over the sea. This would be out of character for me. I would never have gone to the sea except as a child, when my parents would have dipped my toes in and out of the Pacific until I cried.

What are you crying about? they would have asked, but I could never have said.

Despite this, I would go to Tojinbo to gaze out over the sea.

If I were a temporary worker in Japan, my Japanese boyfriend would be the breadwinner. He would *bring home the bacon.*

That's not how we say it here, he'd tell me.

Being the breadwinner would be expected of him. It would be expected of me, as a temporary worker, to go wherever someone might need me, to sit alone in our twelve-tatami apartment until someone did. It would be expected of me, as an American, to laugh too loudly, to touch people who didn't want to be touched, to say *eigo-o hanashimasu ka?* when my Japanese failed.

Please tell me you speak English.

If I were a temporary worker in Japan, the sea and the sky at Tojinbo would be gray the day I went there. There would be no other tourists, no tour guide with a garish flag, just a smattering of rain, or perhaps only the spray of the sea, spattering my glasses.

While I was gazing out over the sea, I would be approached by an older man. If I talked about him later, I wouldn't use his real name. I would call him something like Tanigawa, which, to me, is very Japanese.

It's beautiful, isn't it? he'd say.

Hai, I'd say. *So beautiful.*

If I were a temporary worker in Japan, Tanigawa-san would crouch beside me, chin in his hand. He would talk about innocuous things, such as the weather or the price of square watermelons nowadays.

He'd say: *In my day, we didn't even have square watermelons,* and I would laugh too loudly and tap him on the shoulder.

He'd say: *Are there square watermelons in America?*

Oval, I'd say, and make the shape with my hands. *Only oval.*

If I were a temporary worker in Japan, Tanigawa-san would say: *You shouldn't jump, you know.*

I'd say: *I wasn't going to jump.*

Tanigawa-san would look out over the sea. He'd tell me about all the people he had stopped from jumping before. He would say he'd seen enough of them to know. They all had the same look on their faces.

You know, he'd say, but I would shake my head.

And these people, he'd say, these people who had come here to die— he helped them. He'd say he could help me, too.

I'm not going to jump, I'd say.

Tanigawa-san would smile, but it would be the kind of smile my parents gave me when we drove away from the Pacific Ocean, promising me ice cream to stop my tears. He'd pat my shoulder.

That's good, he'd say. *That's good.*

If I were a temporary worker in Japan, I would walk along the rocky path with Tanigawa-san back to the train station. The rocks would be wet with sea spray. I would look back at the gray sky, the gray sea.

Tanigawa-san would take both of my hands in his. *If there's anything I can do to help.*

There's nothing, I'd say. *I don't need any help.*

Except that I would say it wrong, so it would come out more like this: *You can't help me.*

Tanigawa-san would squeeze my hands tightly in his.

I just wanted to see the ocean, I would say. *I have to go.*

I would ride the train away, without looking back. I would whisper the Japanese word for help to myself: *Tasukete. Tasukete.*

If I were a temporary worker in Japan, my Japanese boyfriend would be waiting for me in our twelve-tatami apartment. He would say: *You smell like you've been to the sea.*

He would say: *How was it, the sea?*

I met an old man there, I would say. *He thought I wanted to jump. Isn't that funny?*

My boyfriend would laugh too loudly and tap my shoulder. He'd say: *It's very funny.*

He'd say: *Yes, it's very funny.*

Whale Watch Chaperone Application 17.B

KAITLYN ANDREWS—RICE

I, <u>Karin Hammond</u>, (MOTHER)/FATHER/GUARDIAN of <u>Sally Hammond</u>, wish to chaperone <u>Birch Lane Elementary</u> whale watch. By submitting this application, I agree to the following terms and conditions:

WHEREAS, Mammalease, Inc., certifies that, per the Ocean Act of 2051, all WhaleSynths™ seen on a federally mandated whale watch are meant to keep the mystery alive and to preserve the sanctity, magic, etc. of childhood.

WHEREAS, MOTHER agrees to refrain from unnecessary, unauthorized, and/or negligent handling of the facts, TRUTH, as defined by Department of Education ("DoE") Childhood Innocence Directive 7046.1.

WHEREAS, MOTHER agrees that disclosure of the TRUTH could cause irreparable damage to children and/or MOTHER. MOTHER must refrain from disclosing TRUTH to other people's children unless there is an unavoidable emergency[1]. In the case of an emergency, MOTHER agrees to generate ALTERED-TRUTHs as appropriate.

WHEREAS, MOTHER agrees that Mammalease, Inc., will not be held responsible in the event of TRUTH disclosure related to the extinction of fully aquatic placental marine mammals, TRUE WHALEs. Children may become distraught when informed of the TRUTH after being told an ALTERED-TRUTH (e.g., WhaleSynths™, Tooth Fairy, Santa, Easter Bunny, Caucasian Jesus, etc.).

APPLICATION QUESTIONNAIRE

1. Did MOTHER see a TRUE WHALE prior to the Ocean Act of 2051? y/n

   If yes, please explain:

If the only thing MOTHER can remember about TRUE WHALEs is her fifth-grade whale watch, which occurred the day after Genny, BEST FRIEND, confessed to being in love with Son of God, JESUS, that's fine.

Start with BEST FRIEND.

Start with JESUS.

BEST FRIEND, who had fallen for JESUS, sat on a shell-shaped bench rocking back and forth in a dramatic exaggeration of the boat's sway in the tipsy Atlantic.

BEST FRIEND said: God knows every drop of H20 in this ocean!

MOTHER said: OK!

Perhaps it was OK with a question mark? Or congrats with an exclamation point? Or good for him? Good for capital-H-him? We note that responsible party, MOTHER, cannot commit to a verbatim account of what happened when she was twelve. Therefore, the transcript above and below may include inaccuracies, and further investigation may be required.

On the day of MOTHER's whale watch, BEST FRIEND, recent lover of JESUS, "said":

I am asking for safe passage on this whale watch. I am asking that we see at least one of God's amazing creatures. God will show us because I am asking. Don't take it for granted!

MOTHER nodded, but for what? For why?

Prior to this field trip, BEST FRIEND had begun acting strange, obsessive even, what with the faux diamond cross around her neck, which she gazed at longingly during Advanced Placement lessons about the Battle of Fort Sumter[2]. At the same time, MOTHER OF BEST FRIEND became obsessed with hand washing, hand soap, and general cleanliness. MOTHER OF BEST FRIEND pinched pennies for overpriced bottles of soap, one Strawberry Kiwi Burst™ and one Tahitian Vanilla Sunset™, both with microbeads (ban on such microbeads having gone into effect on September 22, 2016, through Article 23: Impact on Rivers, Ponds, Oceans, Streams, and Other Waterbodies Irreversible and Permanent). When the expensive soap ran dry, MOTHER OF BEST FRIEND refilled the hourglass-shaped bottles with the type of industrial pink soap found in schools, libraries, and other government institutions.

1A. Does MOTHER really think this detail re: the soap is relevant? y/n

  If yes, please explain:

MOTHER feels, noting the strong discouragement of feelings related to WhaleSynths™, that symbolism is pertinent. Symbolism is herein defined as: nothing is what it seems, for generic soap in a fancy bottle is still generic soap, for WhaleSynths™ designed to mimic TRUE WHALEs are still WhaleSynths™. Does an organism become un-extinct simply because a conglomerate—using funds from the guy who invented Quip™ and unquestionably questionable Middle Eastern benefactors—finally creates the once-impossible, morally circumspect simulated organism?

2. Can MOTHER function as a responsible chaperone? y/n

  If no, please explain:

Is it possible that MOTHER, who waited until the acceptable age of thirty-two[3] to be with child, remains largely scared? Scared of her daughter? Of herself? Of other mothers? Of protecting too much or not protecting enough?

If MOTHER is indeed scared, she may feel that explaining TRUE WHALEs to her child(ren) is too difficult. We encourage parents, especially MOTHER, to avoid bringing too much baggage (of the figurative and/or literal variety) to a whale watch featuring WhaleSynths™. The fact that WhaleSynths™ are scientifically engineered, meticulously constructed replicas of TRUE WHALEs should have no impact on a child's educational experience. Furthermore, all 7-Seas ships are equipped with WhaleSynths™ Vocalization Pods™, a whole-body immersion therapy inspired by a TRUE WHALE's lyrical language.

3. Has MOTHER ever generated ALTERED-TRUTHs to protect loved ones? y/n

   If no, please explain in great detail:

The following is the recorded recollection of MOTHER, duly recorded in DiRee[4]. Therefore, its accuracy can be neither confirmed nor denied:

    Genny's extremely clean mom kidnapped me.
    Instead of taking us to that movie she announced
    a pit stop. In my house, pit stops mean drive-
    thru for Diet Cokes. In Genny's house, pit stops

apparently mean Jesus, which means a strip mall off 95. "We're going to church, girls. Buckle up," Genny's mom said, and she pushed us into their minivan, which always smells like English muffins, which I hate and which made me throw up the one time Genny's mom got us Egg McMuffins. Now Genny's mom despises, avoids, detests, etc. fast-food chains, calls them places quote unquote where you can get buckets of sinner's soda and other awful crud, home cooks everything, proudly refers to herself as a homemaker, and cries from joy about the home cooking and homemaking. Apparently when you find Jesus, you find all kinds of passions for ironing and pie baking. Anyway, Genny's mom, who promised us a blockbuster with my future hubby Ryan Rain, took us to a strip mall instead. Between Paula's Pawn Shop and Karla's Gifts and More Store is where Genny's whole family apparently found salvation.

I don't get it. At all. Last week Genny and I performed a lyrical dance in sequined unitards to a song with the lyrics, "Bounce, bounce on that flounce, flounce, hey, hey, Straye[5]!"

This week Genny's fam kidnaps me in the name of Jesus. Would anyone find me? Would my Christmas-celebrating Jewish dad and my kinda Catholic, Unitarian Universalist-flirting mom even know where to look? Had Genny's mom asked their permission for this insane-in-the-membrane field trip?

Inside the strip mall church, which was basically a tiny basement with a super-disturbing bleeding Jesus thingie, a big woman with limp hair and an actual limp began to sway. Her cylindrical body jiggled as she moved between folding chair pews. Raising her floppy arms, she sang "saved in the breath of Jesus" over and over until the entire room, with the exception of moi, joined. Then the big woman with limp hair and a limp, with the floppy arm fat Mom doesn't want to get, fell to the ground squirming and moaning, her legs bucking around, her body like a beached whale.

Was she having a seizure? No, no, nope! She was "slain in the spirit"! That's actually what Genny's mom said after. Like it was totally normal for a grown woman to have a Jesus-seizure. Then she handed us post-spirit slaying refreshments: kiddie-sized cups of Hi-C (ew) and stale popcorn from a convenience store across the parking lot. I guess men and women flip-flopping around on a nasty carpet, speaking in rhythmic nonsense only, like, a scientist can decode, are a good and an inspirational thing. But then, as I wished for buttered popcorn, for a jug of Diet Coke, for the ability to be anywhere but here, I realized three Very Important Things: 1. Genny's family scares me. A fuckton. 2. Jesus is a total fraud: he can turn water into wine but can't turn Hi-C into Diet Coke? 3. Someday Genny'll find out this Jesus stuff is way wrong and be so upset. Or someday I'll find out she's right, and I'll drown in a massive bucket of sinner's soda. UGH. Genny's my

BFF, but her family? Creepcity. I dunno if I'll

even go to her sleepover party next week[6].

As illustrated above, MOTHER, perhaps hysterical with recollection of BEST FRIEND, is not in the right state of mind to fully disclose her prior experience with TRUE WHALEs and/or ALTERED-TRUTHs.

4. Is MOTHER hysterical? y/n

If yes, we remind MOTHER that she may have been one of the last generations to witness a TRUE WHALE as nature (common name: God) intended. Therefore, MOTHER is most unique, having seen the world both as it was meant to be and as the government, corporations, and wealthy benefactors have spent unprecedented resources to re-create.

5. Did MOTHER see a TRUE WHALE on aforementioned field trip? y/n

If yes, would MOTHER please explain herself?

Post-prayer BEST FRIEND ran yelping to the rusty boat's bow, followed by giddy classmates high on fried fish and whale-shaped creamsicles.

BEST FRIEND jumped up and down, pointing to what BEST FRIEND swore was a tail lobbing in the ocean.

6. Was it a TRUE WHALE, MOTHER? y/n

7. MOTHER, was it? y/n

8. Or was it simply a rock, endlessly covered and uncovered by ocean froth, unmoved and unchanged? y/n

9. Does MOTHER really think this has anything to do with whales? y/n

Yes.

APPENDIX

Approved TRUTH-TELLING Emergencies

- Malfunctioning WhaleSynths™, including but not limited to BlubberPanel™ rupture, extreme oily discharge, excessive rusting, mechanical failure, and/or loss of buoyancy

- Loss of photo opportunity

- Loss of child and/or chaperone

- Photograph documentation of WhaleSynths™ malfunction and/or loss of child and/or chaperone

ENDNOTES

[1] See appendix for list of approved emergencies.

[2] After the storm Vulcan in 2022, Fort Sumter was placed in the Civil War Protection Trust. In 2038, Environment Holdings acquired the Civil War Protection Trust. Environment Holdings owns a controlling interest in Mammalease, Inc., and the intellectual property covering WhaleSynths™.

[3] Thirty-two is on the cusp of Advanced Maternal Age (common name: older woman of child-bearing years, may have child with issues because MOTHER is selfish/wanted career).

[4] An obsolete diary app since replaced by Memchips, a brain add recently approved by the FDA.

[5] According to historical documentation and musical recordings kept by the Musical Registrar of America, "Straye" was a slang term meaning "your boyfriend's/girlfriend's ex who is now your BFF." In context, one might use "Straye" like this: "We talked about his weird tongue and now she's, like, my Straye for life."

[6] After MOTHER OF BEST FRIEND forced pre-sleeping-bag prayers and gave out GirlBibles™ as party favors, MOTHER left sleepover party early and never spoke to BEST FRIEND again.

There Once Was a Man

AFTER THE NARRATIVE OF ARTHUR GORDON PYM OF NANTUCKET
BY EDGAR ALLAN POE

KELCEY PARKER ERVICK

MEN WASH UP ON THE shore: dead, almost dead, hungry. They all have stories. She thinks she has a story, too, even if she doesn't yet know what it is. Surely it has to do with the light. Not the absence of darkness, but the pure sliver of light that beams from the lighthouse into a sea of darkness. She thinks of the night sky like this sometimes: a sea of darkness. But if the sky is a sea, does that make the wild sea a sky? In daylight she can see the sea, and she calls it the sky. The boats with their winged sails fly across the sky. She and her aunt live alone at the edge of the wet, wet sky, beneath a starlit sea. How did she get here?

There once was a man from Nantucket.

Let's say his name was Arthur Gordon Pym. Let's say he wrote a narrative of his adventures at sea. That he left out very little about the parts of the ship, the geography of the seas, the nature of his desperate and dehydrated dreams, the quantities and types of food available, the deaths of shipmates, the cannibalism, the encounters with savages, the cryptic markings on the chasm rocks, the escape, and the quality and texture of the air as he sailed toward the southernmost pole.

But he left out a lot of other things, this man from Nantucket. Let's say that just before these adventures, Arthur Gordon Pym knew a girl. That he got her up in a certain way. Not knowing what to do about the girl and her situation, he found himself overcome with strange desires. He became consumed by "visions of shipwreck and famine; of death and captivity among barbarian hordes." And so he left the girl and the situation, and he hopped on a ship, the Grampus.

Be careful what you wish for, man from Nantucket.

Let's say the girl he knew gave birth to a girl. That the girl he knew died giving birth to a baby girl, and that this daughter was turned over to her aunt. Let's say that the aunt was a lighthouse keeper, one of the few women on the job.

Growing up at the edge of the sea, the girl reads. Not folk tales, which seem filled with motherless girls like her. No, she reads of adventures on land and sea. She reads of Gulliver, Robinson Crusoe, King Arthur, Robin Hood, and Don Quixote. Her aunt's small house is filled with books that the men from the ships leave behind.

The girl imagines that the rocks that jut into the water are the bow of her ship, which she sails into the seas. That she is headed on a seafaring adventure. When boats appear, they are coming toward her ship for help, or to trade information. When supplies are low, she eyes her aunt's thick arms and neck like: food. That is what adventurers do.

Then again: she is the savage, the native, the heathen. On the wall of the lighthouse, she uses a rock to scratch stories and stick figures. She speaks her own language, worships the all-powerful lighthouse.

Men wash up on the shore: dead, almost dead, hungry.

From her books she knows the men will measure her, take note of her clothing, and inquire about her gods. She will point to the lighthouse; she will bow down before it. They will tell her about their God, the one with the capitalized G. He is in threes: father, son, holy spirit. Omnipotent, omnipresent, omniscient. Who is this amazing deity? she will ask. Where does he live? Why, he is everywhere, they will tell her. But I can't see him, she will say, frightened, for this God is too much like her own father, whom she has also never seen. She will run to the top of the lighthouse and scream and scream.

The men stay for a night or two, until the weather clears, until the ship is repaired, until the next ship appears. She follows the men so she can take things from their pockets and satchels. A magnifying glass, a compass, a book, a bottle of something that burns her throat when she drinks. To be a girl is to be not quite unseen—for the men see her, tell jokes about her girlness, predict her bland future—but rather to be invisible. As they laugh and say how many children she will have, what sort of husband, she searches their bags and pockets. She knows they are wrong about her future.

She spies scrimshaw. Confiscates it. Later she will rub her fingertips along the images on the whalebone, images of faces and fish, ships and seas she will never know. She steals a knife, which she keeps for the men who come too close, whose drunken eyes leer. She is not always so invisible.

When there are no men, she spends her days listening to the conch shell for its messages and whispering her secrets back into its pearled depths. She catches fish, names them and eats them. Practice.

The girl grows and learns. She follows the aunt up, up, up the spiral steps, lugging buckets of whale oil, and torches the candles and polishes the lenses that cast the light into the darkness. The small flame magnified for miles. She practices each task and embraces the rhythm of up and down, light and darkness. She knows that others go to church to worship a capitalized God, but she enters her god and worships from within. When the aunt is gone, she carves more stories on its darkened walls.

The aunt doesn't believe in God anymore, not since He took away her husband and son. This was before the girl arrived, but not long before, and the aunt has forever connected the girl's arrival with their departures. *Devoted Husband*, it says on the larger tombstone behind the house. *Beloved Son*, reads the smaller one beside it, *Died March 6, 1827. Lived 1 y. 2 m. 9 d.*

In the sand at the foot of the lighthouse, the girl uses a stick to compose predictions for her tombstone. She tries out a series of dates for her death. Her birthdate stays the same, in 1828, but her death date varies. Maybe it will be February 21, 1871. Or August 20, 1859. Or any of the thousands of days in between. Or after. Or even before. She tries out inscriptions: *Orphan Girl. Castaway. Cannibal. She Kept the Light.*

[In another version of the story, she would not spend her youth writing tombstone messages. She would have two parents and a sister to perform skits with. She would have her father's last name, not her aunt's husband's name. She would go to school and become a teacher, or something.]

[In still another version, she would have been a boy. But actually that is not another version. That is another story altogether.]

Growing up, the daughter has two questions: Who is my mother? Who is my father? As to the former, the aunt says: My sister, God rest her soul. As to the latter, the aunt says nothing. The aunt slips up only once, without even knowing it, but that is all the daughter needs. The girl keeps the name of her father alight in her mind just as her aunt keeps the light on for the sailors. *Pym. Pym. Pym.*

The name is both foreign and familiar. There once was a man from Nantucket.

One night, the light burns out, a ship wrecks near their shore, and a man dies in the darkness. Did the aunt forget to add more oil? Did she do it on purpose? Either way, after that, the aunt turns. Becomes a different

sort of aunt. She spends more time writing in the log book and increasingly leaves the lighthouse duties to the girl. The girl, who is beginning to think of herself as a woman, reads the aunt's log, and instead of weather reports and accounts of the men who wash up, all is gloom: *Nothing but sorrow, without and within. This is not a fit place for anyone to live in. Oh, what a place. All misery and darkness. This is such a dreary place to be in all alone.*

All alone? If the aunt is all alone, that must make the girl all alone too. She climbs to the top of the lighthouse and screams.

From the top of the lighthouse, the girl who is beginning to think of herself as a woman looks out to the sea and thinks about her father. *Pym.* Familiar, foreign. She can't place it. Nor can she dwell on it. The light is her duty now. The aunt is her duty now. If the light goes out the ships will run aground. Nights, she can't sleep, thinking about the light. She peers out her window to make sure it still glows. When she does sleep, her dreams are of the light. It is always dimming, always receding. She can't get to it in time. She cries out. *Pym!*

The aunt is raving mad when the men wash up on the shore. One man is dead, another is almost dead, a third is very hungry.

The girl, upon seeing the third, finds herself, despite her breakfast of cooked eggs, suddenly hungry too. She is used to feeling love for the dead ones, whose puckered and bloated faces are like scrimshaw that tell stories of their now-finished lives. She occasionally feels love for the almost-dead ones, if only because they give her something to do other than lighthouse duties, such as bringing them water and blankets until the doctor arrives. But when they return from almost-death and can speak again, they smell rotten, and she cannot love them anymore.

Is it love she feels for the hungry man? It is her nineteenth summer, and she longs to feel real love for a living man. She tests the idea, but it fails. No, she feels hunger.

It is late at night when she makes herself alone with him. They are under the moon that shines like a light on the night's dark sea. She cannot see that part of him, but she is hungry and she touches it. And when she does, she thinks of a lighthouse. Rising up between sea and sky, sky and sea. She lets go with her hand and then. She can feel the light in her darkness.

[In one version of the story this is how she comes to have her own daughter. How, even years later when the chickens have been washed into the sea by a strong storm and there are no more eggs for her or her daughter to eat, she never feels hunger again.]

[In another version of the story, this is how she comes to leave the lighthouse. She calls her hunger love, and she follows the hungry man to the city, where she loves and hungers for her husband and children in quiet desperation; where, nights, she dreams of the light and stormy seas.]

In this version, the hungry man grows satiated by meals eaten with the babbling aunt, nights with the girl. But the girl's hunger only grows. She begins to fear it will never be satisfied. She wants the man, but he is not enough. She wants him to ask about her god, to learn her language, interpret her carvings.

Instead she says: Take me with you. Take me on an adventure at sea. I want shipwreck and famine, death and captivity!

The man laughs, and it is only then that she realizes she is nothing but a girl. Not even a savage. She has never been a savage, just a girl who nurses men back to life. Just a girl who keeps the light bright so the men can go on their adventures.

Still: the girl fears her hunger, her own savage nature. Maybe she will eat him.

One night she speaks the name of her father. Pym? the hungry man says. Pym, she says. Of Nantucket? he says. She doesn't know. I've heard his tale, he says. He has a tale? Tell me!

But the hungry man doesn't remember exactly. Something about mutiny and cannibals. Did he go to the center of the earth? the hungry man wonders aloud, gnawing on a chicken bone, but can't quite recollect. Is he alive? she asks, clutching the man's collar. The hungry man can't recall.

January 24, 1848. Hurricane Pym. Devoted daughter.

Whale oil costs more each day, and there are rumors of gold in California. The hungry man boards a ship, sets off on a new adventure. This is how the girl comes to understand the world and its workings. Men come, men go. Women stay put, women go mad. There once was a man, but now he is gone. This is something her mother could have told her if her mother had lived. Women give birth, women die.

After the man leaves, the girl paces and paces. He has a tale, he has a tale. If he has a tale, maybe she has a tale, maybe he wrote about her. Maybe he is alive; maybe she will find him. Inside the house, she takes one book after another from her aunt's shelves, tears them in two, tosses them in the fire. The aunt cries out. Where is it, the girl says. Where?

And then she sees it: *The Narrative of Arthur Gordon Pym of Nantucket.* Had it been there all along?

The seas cease, the birds silence, the aunt dissolves into nothing.

The girl reads.

Let's say you're a man from Nantucket and you've been at sea for months. You didn't have to go to sea at all; adventure just seemed more appealing. No one writes stories about a life at home with a woman and child. But that was before you saw your best friend die and had hunger so strong that you ate the flesh of your sacrificed shipmate. Now you're floating on a canoe, headed toward the South Pole where you've heard tell of an entrance to an inner world and a superior society, and although this sounds fantastic, as in impossible and improbable, you have just seen your two dozen shipmates swallowed by a trap set in the earth by savages, and you barely made it off the island alive, and you are with Peters, the only other survivor, and a native named Nu-Nu who is now dead in your canoe, and you're desperate enough to believe in the wildest story.

Now let's say you are a girl reading this story about a man from Nantucket, and all you can think is: Papa? Is that what I would call you? And: Afterward, in all those years, did you try to find me, Papa?

But her father's story ends before it is actually over (like everything, everything), and no one knows if he made it to the center of the earth,

Meanwhile, men still wash up on the shore: dead, almost dead, hungry.

and it doesn't matter anyway because by then she knows he did not write about her, did not try to find her, probably never thought about her or her mother at all, and she feels the clay of her heart harden. She sets down the book to tend the light. These are the only things she can rely on: darkness, herself. When she returns to the chair and reads in the epilogue about the death of Pym, she is not surprised, and is only slightly moved to know he was alive for the first decade of her life.

The girl is woman now, mentally and emotionally. She has long been a woman physically. She logs her days: the storms, the ships that wreck, the household maintenance, the crabs torn apart by gulls. Sometimes she adds something else in the log, something that has nothing to do with the weather or ship traffic, but there is no one to notice it. She comes to understand her father's writing, her aunt's writing, even the inscrutable symbols of the savages in her father's book: some things get written down, some omitted, some forgotten, others kept deep within. Etched in sand, scratched on scrimshaw.

There once was a man from Nantucket. This is the story of his forgotten daughter.

Gulls and tides. Sometimes you just want quiet. Inside, the house is cold. Sometimes she reads aloud when the aunt, in a moment of lucidity, requests it. She reads *The Narrative of Arthur Gordon Pym of Nantucket.* It always ends the same, with her father sailing toward the South Pole where he sees the large, shrouded white figure. The girl makes up her own final lines in her father's voice: "And as I gazed at the figure, I knew it was the woman I had left behind, holding our daughter in her arms. At last I was returning to them."

But that, she knows, is her own version of the story, not his.

Meanwhile, men still wash up on the shore: dead, almost dead, hungry. The girl keeps a pilfered gun strapped to her leg.

One day there is a Negro. He washes up on the shore alone with a broken boat. He is gaunt, hunched over, and she does not know at first if he is dead, almost dead, or hungry. It is 1851. She knows she should turn him in. She knows she shouldn't. In her father's book, the dark-skinned men are called savages. The new law calls them fugitives.

[In one version of the story, she tricks him into staying long enough that she can alert officials of the nearby town and turn him in. She collects a reward and wonders what to do with it.]

But this is not that version, and this is not her father's book. For when she looks into the man's eyes, with the lighthouse reflecting in them, she understands that he is on an adventure. She gives him food and points him toward the city she's never seen. He thanks her with a voice from the faraway seas, as deep as the skies.

The aunt dies. The girl digs the grave herself, writes in the fresh earth with a stick—just one word, *AUNT*—and stabs the stick in the ground.

Some days she thinks of the Negro and hopes he got where he was going. Some days she thinks where he was going might also be bad for him, that he will encounter savages. She wonders whether there is anywhere on this earth he can go.

Other days she thinks of the hungry man, who devoured her so long ago. There once was a man. She should have eaten him.

Her father had not written about her, not in his famous narrative, anyway. She wishes the savages had killed him with the rest. Then he wouldn't have written anything at all.

Often she wonders, what if she didn't light the light? All the men in the world would wash up on her dark shore. She would set a trap and kill them all.

March 6, 1900. Eater of men.

The older she gets, the more she thinks of her girlhood when she believed she was a savage. She makes mandalas out of shells in the sand. Or forms the shells into large letters, words for the birds to carry into the clouds.

She puts a message in a bottle, tosses the bottle in the sea. The waves roll it back to her. The sky is the sea, the sea is the sky.

In the log book she makes up words, phrases, even letters. She sketches symbols like the savages in her father's story.

Let's say it's your job to decipher, to tell the story of the woman who kept the light. Surely she has one.

May 7, 2075. Oldest Woman in the World.

Tonight there are such gales. The gales will bring more men: dead, almost dead, hungry. But for now, no one arrives, and supplies are running low. She can't see any stars. The entire world is house, tower, sand, sea. She takes her father's book and climbs to the top of the lighthouse. She lights the wick, tears out a page of the book, and touches it to the flame. She dips another page in whale oil and lights it, startled by its fury. She lights another. The fiery pages gather at her feet, and, although she is burning the evidence, wants it turned to ash, there is something she can no longer ignore. For years she has believed the book was her father's story, but now, as its pages catch the hem of her dress on fire, she confronts an idea she has resisted for years: that her father never existed at all.

That there never was a man from Nantucket. That he was only ever a story.

And if that is true (for it is), what does that make her?

Alone at the top of the fiery lighthouse, she screams and screams.

Somewhere in the distant sea, there is a man on a ship who sees an unusually bright light on the shore. It fills him with hunger.

The Giant's Needle

ALLISON WYSS

M Y BROTHER HAD SEVEN SONS. The first was him again, except not as tall or as clever, and the spark in his eyes was not as bright. The second was a washed-out version of the first. The third a washed-out version of the second. And so on.

I, being a woman and a glorious one, determined to have a daughter, and so that her spark would be bright I decided to have only one.

She was born bright and strong, even more than I and much wiser. I don't know where she acquired the extra spark. Perhaps she stole it from her father, long forgotten except in her light. Or perhaps from the midwife, who was big in my view, between my legs, but disappeared. Or maybe my daughter snatched it from the night itself. For who would notice if a single star snuffed out?

When she was grown, and all my brother's seven sons were grown before her, my brother hoped there would be a union among them. I was skeptical of the marriage of cousins but trusted my daughter to make a wise decision.

The oldest and tallest and brightest of my brother's sons approached her. My daughter promised to marry him if he would bring her the sewing needle of the giant that lived beneath the mountain. The needle was sharp and long like a sword and highly prized by the giant.

I did not know if she most wanted the brother dead or wanted to possess the needle, but it was the former that occurred. When his light was extinguished, some of it passed to the second son of my brother and the rest distributed among the other five.

The second son approached my daughter, and, as with the first, she agreed to marry him if he could bring her the giant's needle.

This second son tried to reason with my daughter. The giant's hand was large, he said, and strong. While the giant lived, the hand would not release the needle. While the giant lived, it would take but a flick from its weakest finger to kill a man. It would take but a quick stitch from the needle to pierce his heart.

My daughter said nothing, but her eyes shone brightly. The second son sought the giant under the mountain, and in trying to take the needle he was killed. His brightness was distributed among his younger brothers, and perhaps a bit went elsewhere.

My daughter sought the third son and demanded that he steal the needle for her. She demanded that he kill the giant if he had to, or that he slice off the hand that held the sword-length needle.

But the third son had no interest in marriage or giants or sword-like needles. He took to the sea and became a sailor, then a pirate. It is said he buried a treasure on every shore, and that on each shore the treasure increased sevenfold by the time of his return. But that is a different story.

The fourth son, at my brother's bidding, approached my daughter and was given the same task as the first. He failed, and his spark passed to his younger brothers. They glowed. But never as bright as the first, for each time the spark was passed some of it was lost.

Who took it? Was it my daughter, growing wiser, but somehow not dulling with the years?

The fifth son followed the third and was lost at sea. My daughter's roars to bring the giant's sewing needle were lost in his ears as the waves crashed over his head and the fish consumed him.

The sixth son took to the church. It was in the confessional that my daughter begged for not only the giant's needle but also both of the giant's hands and both of the giant's feet. I saw that her wisdom was warping. The sixth son did not comply but forgave her for asking.

It is only when we reach the seventh son that the tale gets interesting. He passed my daughter his own hands and feet, cut from his arms and legs in jagged lines. He roped the shoreline of the ocean into a leash and used his own sword as a needle to string it with beads of rocks and shells and starfish. Then he prayed the ocean like a rosary, bead by dripping bead. He wrapped the rope of ocean around my daughter's waist and hung his hands from her ears and his feet from her neck.

When she received the gifts, my daughter laughed. "Why would I marry a man with stumps for arms and legs?"

"Why would I expect it?"

"Fool! Then why would you give me such gifts?"

"Only because I had nothing better to do with them," he said. And he limped away, shining brightly but not as brightly as my daughter, not as brightly as the feet and the hands that hung from her.

The brightness was blinding. I feared it was too much.

Then my daughter did a strange thing. She removed her girdle of ocean and the hands from her ears and the feet from her neck. She strung them into the sky to replace the star that she'd stolen.

Then she returned to my house to live unmarried and to shine brightly forever.

Rehearsed

KATIE YOUNG FOSTER

A FRIEND I USED TO RUN with once a week invited me to her wedding. The ceremony was to be held on the sprawling lawn behind her house. The vows would be spoken at dusk.

When I received the invitation—a short text message accompanying a screen shot of the date and location—it had been almost a year since our last 5 a.m. run. We'd taken time off so I could have a baby. I was, at first, surprised that Sara had invited me, so far from my mind were the hundreds of miles we'd jogged together, the street lamps casting orange pools of light, the puffs of our breath as we'd chatted. *Thinking of you*, Sara's text message had said. *I know this particular time in your life is beautiful but also, of course, very sad. Come if you can.*

The man she was marrying played in a band. I hadn't met him but had often heard Sara describe him in counterpoint to the man she'd been with before. "Liam shows emotion," she'd told me, early in their relationship. We were jogging downhill in a freefall of leaves. It was autumn. I was seven weeks pregnant with my second attempt at a child. All that was left of the first was a vanilla-scented candle, which we burned on the fourteenth of every month. "Genuine emotion," Sara repeated. We pivoted and began the slow ascent up Forrest Street. I listened to the new boyfriend's attributes: Liam reads Dostoevsky. Liam brings her coffee in bed. When Liam asks her opinion, he seems to value what she tells him.

"But I don't know if I'll ever commit again, officially," Sara said.

I'd nodded. It was the first time my friend had implied that she and the other man—the one before Liam, whom she circled around but never named—had been married.

On the evening of the wedding, my husband dropped me off in front of Sara's blue brick bungalow a few minutes late. He was heading to the gym in an attempt to lose the weight he'd gained after my first pregnancy— *grief weight,* we called it. He'd asked if I could go to the wedding alone. I approached the ceremony. Above, strands of lights hung from the branches of pin oaks. Candles burned on wooden benches, which were arranged in alcoves in the shrubbery. As I walked across the grass, the last disc of sun slipped behind the trees. Under an ivy-covered arch, my friend rose up on her toes to kiss her new husband. Sara's cheeks were flushed, her hair threaded with a crown of eucalyptus. The people gathered around them whooped. *Mr. and Mrs.,* someone shouted.

My son stirred against my chest. He was two months old, and I carried him everywhere, snug to my body, wrapped in a cotton sling. The child before him had also been a boy, but that one had favored my husband—black hair, light eyes. This son was blond. I'd named him Noah Richard, after my father. Noah had the habit of sucking his fingers noisily, even while sleeping. Multiple times a day, while my husband was at work, I'd walk past the double mirrors in our hallway. It was a relief to view my son from two perspectives—on me, and apart from me—and to watch the rise and fall of his back as he breathed. I'd stand there and rub his thatch of blond hair, which seemed to me to grow darker, daily, under my hands.

I poured myself a glass of red wine at the drink station. At the edge of the yard, under a white canopy, three farm tables were strewn with periwinkle. Old-fashioned lamps spilled light onto trays with labels such as "jalapeño pickles" and "concord grape pie." Guests had begun to wade through the shadowy yard, heading for seats.

Sara and Liam approached me. Together, they hugged me and laid hands on my son, as if we were the ones to be celebrated. They teased Noah as he sucked his fist.

"Congratulations," I told them. "You two—you're meant for each other."

Sara caught my eye. I touched my son's cheek, and she smiled. I let the moment wash over me, reminded of a morning in November, years ago, when we'd sprinted between two stoplights on Forrest. She'd opened up to me then about her fear of growing old without kids or a dependable partner. "How did this happen?" she'd asked. Her voice had been ragged.

"But you'll find someone else," I'd told her. "You *will*."

My words had sounded hollow, rehearsed, part of a discussion we'd already had, in so many ways, over so many mornings.

"And you'll be given someone, too," she'd responded. I'd stiffened. I was married. No kids, of course, but I was fine. By then, we'd finished our miles and were sitting outside a café, drinking coffee, watching the sun break through the fog on the road. Sara hadn't been speaking to me, exactly—she'd been speaking to her coffee, to her hands, to the cars that whipped past us carrying men and women and the potential for love, to the ambulances that transported children to hospitals, to the grief of un-met strangers, to no one.

*

SARA led me across the lawn to her parents, who were seated in the center of the longest table. Her mother was playing with wax that had dribbled from a candle; she had teeth just like my friend's. Sara's father was already eating. He was barrel-chested, reserved, a Methodist preacher. I sat to their left.

Noah was restless. He was ready to sleep. I readjusted the wrap and wondered if it was too soon to call my husband to pick us up.

"He's sweet," said Sara's mother, without looking up. She rubbed the wax off her fingers. I could hear in her voice a hesitation to get too in-volved, as if her wish to participate fully in the night was tempered by some thought or obstacle she'd hidden from me.

I thanked her and asked where they were from, when they'd arrived. I complimented the ceremony. I could sense the father listening.

"What do you do for a living?" Sara's mother asked.

"Stay-at-home mom," I said. "Freelancing, sometimes."

"Typical," Sara's father interrupted. He tugged at his beard and tried to catch my eye.

"Pardon?" I said.

"I just mean that you get cut in half, as a parent. Working. Breastfeeding. Forgetting this, losing that. It all gets to be so much." He tapped Noah on the ear. "Is this little man your first?"

I leaned away from him and didn't answer. A hush fell over the tables. Sara and Liam were standing.

"Dad," Sara called down the row. "Dad, will you say a prayer?"

Her father stood. The rest of us clasped our hands. The wood grain on the table's surface was scarred, rough under my elbows. Noah gave a feeble wail. I bowed my head and kissed his hair.

The words my friend's father spoke were simple, traditional—an invocation of happiness, of life-long blessings, of faithfulness. The prayer became a toast. He lifted his wine glass to his daughter.

"To Sara," he said. "To Lance."

The words came back to us, an echo: *Sara, Lance.*

Darkness entered the lamp-lit yard then. It passed through the white plastic canopy and settled onto the faces of those who had gathered. We became statues or silhouettes. The periwinkles gave off the stench of raw meat. The bride sat frozen. Her father seemed unable to go on.

The mother stood. "Raise your glasses, please," she instructed.

Once again, we held up our goblets of water and wine. The mother blessed the daughter. She blessed the right man. Down the table, Liam drank deeply, one arm across my friend's back. He kissed her.

After the meal, couples broke off to play games in the yard—glow-in-the-dark badminton, croquet. Sara remained seated. I waited for her to bolt, to head for the night-darkened road. I smoothed Noah's back. I readied myself to follow my friend. It would take two hundred years of grieving, I knew. Two thousand 5 a.m. runs. And always he'd haunt her, the person who'd left her, who stood in the shadow of the person she'd chosen. This night, invoked and invited, he'd crept to the table to dine with her. They'd scraped clean the piecrust. They'd licked the juice of the meat from their elbows, emptied the dregs of their wine into the milky glow of the candles. I shielded Noah from the smoke.

Aftermilk

TARA CAMPBELL

I. Toast

You've got to get to the toaster as soon as it pops, kids. That's the only way to butter the toast soon enough. That's your golden hour for butter, you know, when you can get it on there and spread it out like a tasty blanket of goodness, even straight from the fridge if you forgot to set it out sooner, which you usually do. There's just too much going on sometimes, you know, making sure everyone did their homework and put on pants and found their shoes, making sure the eggs aren't burning, and then you look up and the toaster's popped long ago and the toast is already cooling, and you've missed your window. I'm not blaming you, kids; that's just how it is sometimes, too much to pay attention to at once.

But, kids, on those days when you don't miss your window and you get there in time, you can do magic. That butter goes on the toast quiet as a cat's paws on carpet, and it soaks right in like rain on the beach, and the bread gets as soft as it was the moment it was born, like right when it came out of the oven, and that's when it smelled the best, too, so it's almost like going back and getting a second chance. And then you bite into it, because when you've buttered it like that, who needs jam, and the butter seeps out

on your tongue, sweet and salty and warm, and it's better than anything you've had in your mouth for years.

I'm just saying it's a real shame when you miss that window, kids.

You miss that window, the best you can hope for is that you remembered to put your butter out soon enough, so it can warm up a little. And maybe you even put it close to the toaster for a little melty action, because you found out the hard way the microwave was too much. That's what you call the nuclear option, like that biker Mommy dated after the divorce.

You kids wouldn't remember him. You mostly stayed with your father then.

So no butter dish in the microwave, okay? If you miss the toaster window, you'll just have to scrape little pieces off your stick of butter and dot your slice with them, and if you hurry, your toast will only be dry in patches. And if you don't think about the way it could have flowed like honey had you got there quicker, you won't miss it too much when it doesn't taste as sweet.

Doesn't pay to think too much on the past, kids. Don't cry over spilled milk or cold toast. You just buck up and make do when you miss your window, even if you forget to take the butter out of the fridge first. Then you just grit your teeth and scrape off as thin a sheet of butter as you can, like a surgeon, and transfer that slice to your cold, crunchy toast, which is probably even a little burned because you bumped the dial when you moved the toaster out of the puddle of juice someone spilled—and left on the counter, mind you, like he didn't have hands to clean it up himself— anyway, you moved the toaster out of the juice so you wouldn't electrocute yourself, and then put the plate on top of the toaster for maybe a hint of warmth, because you know—again, from experience—that you can't even put the whole thing in the microwave, toast and all, and use the toast as a butter buffer, because then the bread will get all chewy and stale, just like your second go-around with that biker who was already too much the first time. (Learn from your mistakes, kids, that's all Mommy asks.) So you go ahead and drag that little sheet of butter across dry land, knife screeching like it's raking a chalkboard, until the butter breaks into smaller shards, and shove that rubble across the desert until it rubs down to pebbles, which you finally have to cram into the toast, which you've fractured and flattened by now, so it looks like one of those videos of water frozen into shelves of ice at the shore. Then you think about all the shredded toast you've had to choke down already, and how many more greasy slices of sawdust you'll have to choke down in the years to come, now that it's too late to go back and spread manna on warm, lightly crisp, sweet-smelling bread. But you can't torture yourself, thinking back to those days when you used to catch it just in time, all the time, when it was just you and your radio and your tea, and maybe later you'd head to the market or a café with a friend before your date with the cute law student that night—he was taking you to dinner somewhere you never could have paid for yourself, and frankly neither could he, not at the moment, but both of you knew it would just be a matter of time till he became partner, in more ways than one, or so you thought before everything else happened and you wound up with the other boy who would become your ex—and you weren't worried about a thing because you thought you had all the time in the world.

But look at that, kids. Toast is done. Here's the butter. Hurry up. That's it, see that butter glide? Hear those cat's paws on carpet? Smell that bakery? Quickly now, get it all the way to the edges. Hurry up, before it dries out. Things have a way of crumbling apart when you wait too long.

II. Love and Orange Juice

NEVER get the orange juice with pulp, kids. It's disgusting. If you want pulp, eat an orange. That's the whole point of orange juice, to have just the juice. Don't ever trust a drink you have to chew. Except for Blizzards.

No, we're not going to Dairy Queen for breakfast. Mommy has some standards, no matter what Daddy might say. I know he makes you drink orange juice with pulp when you're at his house. He always knew how much I hated that stuff, but he still kept on buying it. He said I was just being picky, said it was silly to buy more than one kind of OJ and fill up the fridge with doubles. He'd come back from the store with a huge family-size jug of it, to save money, he said, but really it was just because he was . . . Forget it. I know he asks you kids what I say about him.

Anyway, he tried to get me to drink it with pulp, saying it was healthier, like how all the vitamins from vegetables are in the peel, but I'd just use my fork and lift all those nasty sacs out of there until it was drinkable. Drove him crazy. Even when we had both in the fridge, sometimes I'd be running late and not exactly looking, and I'd pour myself half a glass of that pulped-up sludge before I realized what I was doing, and he always got bent out of shape if I asked him to drink it for me, 'cause he'd already had his by then and said he'd be pissing orange with all the extra juice I made him drink. So I said fine, I'd pour it out, and that about made him blow his top. "Prodigal" was his word. What does that mean? It means a person who doesn't want to chew on a glass full of slimy juice bags.

You don't mind it? Well, that's nice of you, trying not to hurt Daddy's feelings like that. You kids always were kind, you got that from me. Like when he forgot things, which he always did, I didn't always rub his nose in it, you know. In fact, I even told him why I hate OJ with pulp, told him more than once, but he never seemed to remember it when he hit the juice aisle in the grocery store and came home with a carton of nightmares. Well, "nightmares" is a bit strong, but definitely bad memories. Because here's the lesson, kids: always eat breakfast before you start in on the screwdrivers.

It's a drink, kids. Mommy wasn't always as smart as she is now. I made some questionable decisions when I was young, and it's your job to learn from them. See, there was a tradition in high school—you've got a long way to go before then, kids, but you should still hear this. This tradition was called Senior Skip Day. It was in the spring, when the teachers were still teaching, but the kids were just about full up on learning. It was always the second Friday in May, so everyone knew when it was, even the kids who weren't seniors yet. Well, one year, when I was one of those underclassmen, a friend and I decided to join in on Senior Skip Day—but we didn't know where any parties were or anything, so it just turned out to be Two Sophomore Girls Skip Day. So we went over to another girl's house, and turns out she had a party right there under her bed in the form of a fifth of Smirnoff. That's vodka, kids, a nasty, nasty kind of alcohol that looks like water but is anything but.

Long story short, kids, we got those screwdrivers wrong that morning. A real screwdriver is vodka plus probably more orange juice than we were using, plus not on an empty stomach at ten in the morning. We got it all wrong, and as a consequence Mommy got sick, real sick, and it turns out that orange pulp is not so easy to wipe from the floors or from the memory. So ever since then, orange juice with pulp is not how Mommy wants to start her day. And Daddy knows that, because I've told him more than once, and, really, why was pulp more important to him than making his wife happy?

Anyway, don't tell him I said that, kids; he'll just get upset. But let this be a lesson to you, and it's not just about orange juice. Whatever your pulp is in life, bc it ambition or religion or where to live or how many kids to have, or whether to have them at all, never stay with someone who doesn't respect your feelings on it. Not that they have to give in, but if you can't even have equal cartons in the fridge, kids, it's time to pack your bags and go somewhere you can have your own fridge for a change, your own fridge with your own stuff you put there with your own hard work. Because you've always been able to do it, you just didn't know it because you'd always been told you'd never be able to do it on your own.

Don't ever fall for that line, kids. You deserve something out of life, and you can accomplish anything you put your minds to. And you should never be ashamed of following your own goals, large or small. Even if it's something as simple as sitting at your own table in the morning quiet and sipping on a nice, cool glass of orange juice without pulp.

III. Aftermilk

KIDS, I've eaten way too many bowls of slush in my life, and I don't want the same for you. So listen: don't walk away from your cereal once you've poured the milk. Just don't.

You may think you can have it all, wrinkle-free laundry from the dryer and a delicious bowl of Mini-Wheats, but that's an illusion. You hear that buzzer, you block it out or you'll be walking back to a bowl of Pablum with jagged icebergs of wheat sticking up as if they'd tried to claw their way out of the brew.

And don't open the mail after you pour, kids. Don't even look at the mail. Because let me tell you, one phone call about an erroneous charge on your credit card and you'll come back to a swamp full of slimy, bloated Kix corpses you'll have to shovel into your squawker one spoonful after another. It doesn't help that they were stale to begin with. Family size may be cheaper, but it's a heavy price to pay when it's just you and your roommate.

Yes, this was before I met Daddy, before I had you two.

Of course you always have to eat it. It's not like you have money to burn, like you can just throw that nasty goop down the disposal. It's not like you can buy the actual brand names, either. Momma didn't always have Post and Kellogg's in her house, kids. The stars of her shelves were Kroger and Freddy's, or whatever chain store happened to be on her bus line.

Yes, kids, it's nice that we can have Lucky Charms now. So why aren't you eating them? Milk's poured, clock's ticking, school bus is on the way. Didn't you hear a word I said?

You learn early to avoid the puffs and the flakes. You learn soon enough to stick with the clusters, the granolas. They might just have a little crunch left by the time you're done holding your roommate's hair back while she throws up—morning sickness, and you knew that bastard Randy was gonna cut bait as soon as he caught wind of it, and she'd have to move back in with her parents, and you'd have to find another roommate, and sure enough, that's exactly what happened. So always use a condom, kids, and stick with your clusters and granolas.

And know that even Grape-Nuts are no match for certain phone calls. Because sometimes that phone rings, and you think you're just going to pick up for a quick chat with your boyfriend, and by the time you hang up, you've got no more boyfriend because he doesn't believe you when you swear you haven't been sneaking money out of his wallet, when all you had to do was ask. And maybe he's right, because you've been pretending you can afford real Grape-Nuts, and genuine Cheerios and actual Special K, and all just to make him think you had it together enough to buy name brands, but all you have left now is a heaping portion of room-temperature fiber stew.

No, kids, that wasn't Daddy. That was before Mommy met Daddy. But let that be a lesson to you, it doesn't pay to lie. It's not nice to lie, even though everyone does it sometimes. Sometimes you have to, like when you plan a surprise party and you can't tell the person before it happens. Or when you two ask what you're getting for your birthdays and I say, "I don't know." You don't *really* want to know, do you?

I didn't think so. See, sometimes people tell little lies to make other people feel better. Remember when your friend Tina got that crazy haircut, but you both told her it looked good so she wouldn't feel bad? You said the other kids teased her, but you two were nice to her even though you don't really like her.

Those types of lies aren't really lies, they're more like *kindnesses*. Like, it's a kindness when your parents say school simply wasn't the place where you could show your best strengths, or when your friends say sure, you could be a star, you just have to want it bad enough. It's a kindness when agent after agent tells you they'd love to sign you, but producers wouldn't know what to do with your kind of beauty. It's a kindness when your friends say how inspiring it is that you keep chasing your dreams, despite everything. It's a kindness when the guy you're dating, a regular where you waitress, asks you to marry him shortly after the condom breaks, says he was going to ask you anyway. And it's a kindness when you say yes. But then you think maybe kindnesses aren't always that great after all, because somehow all those kindnesses led to a bunch of meanness, and now Mommy and Daddy don't live together anymore.

But, kids, don't misunderstand me: All that kindness, and even the meanness, was all worth it in the end, because look what Mommy got out of it. I got you! I could never have imagined finding something as beautiful as you two on my path of little white lies. And that's not just another kindness, kids. I really mean it.

Listen. Hear the clock chiming? You've got ten minutes to finish up and catch the school bus. Go learn something. Pay attention to Teacher like your lives depend on it. And remember, no failsafe is safe from failure, but even if you mess up, you can still salvage something beautiful out of life.

But first, finish your cereal, kids. Go on. Eat every last spoonful before it all turns to mush.

My Name Is Kit Tucker and I Exist in Sound

JUSTINE CHAN

I KNOW THIS BECAUSE I RAN into a blind saxophone player standing on a patch of blue salt on the side of the snowy street, near the Picasso, playing "Girl from Ipanema," and he stopped and said, "I think I know you from somewhere. I know that voice." He was old and parched, in a patched-up suit, with sunglasses over his eyes and a fedora on his head, and I think he was God. Only God has that sort of taste in fashion, so humble and bare bones, and that raspy, delicious gospel voice. I don't believe in God or Jesus, really, but I don't believe either of them would wear sandals. This is Chicago, I would tell Him. But I don't think I was even talking with Him to begin with. I think I was talking to myself, the way I always do when I'm walking back to the train by myself, and I might have gone quiet, the way I do when I approach people. Not that I care what they think, but I care that they might hear my thoughts and try to psychoanalyze me because everyone tries to and I'm flattered, but, guys, I'm only one person. And I try not to be lonely. That is why I talk to myself. I don't know if God knows that, but I would like to take God out to dinner at a really expensive and fancy restaurant, like Katsu. He would have to tuck away His saxophone in a green velvet-lined case, and I would be very happy thinking of that metal staying warm in the velvet. I would buy him a CTA card if He didn't have one already, and we would ride the bus or the subway. At least the true L stations in the open air have little standing pockets with a heat lamp blazing where God and I could huddle and stay warm, but the more exciting thing would be actually *sitting* next to God or *standing* next to him while we rock and lean in these rattling metal boxes leaking steam and clanging through tunnels. It doesn't matter if it's a bus or a subway, I think. I am not so partial. But when we get to a low, nondescript brick strip of small restaurants, I will know we're close, and I'll let God pull the yellow cord for our stop or whatever makes him feel happy, and we will sit right at the sushi bar, where I ordinarily would not sit, but that is the only place to sit at Katsu. Even if God is not really God but just a blind, homeless old man who plays the saxophone, He will like sitting at the bar because Katsu, the man himself, will be there making the sushi just beyond reach and sight. At the right angle, you can watch the sharp knives slice through spreads of fish, the white and red meats, like butter. Everything is a sleek black, from the wood of the bar to the plates and the cups, all faintly lit right behind Katsu. There is something secret and sweet about sitting so close to the fish. I will order the combo plate—one for each of us—and Katsu will nod approvingly, and God will nod approvingly, but I will wonder if either of them is real, if I am sitting by myself again in Katsu because I do not want to go home to my wife. But that moment will pass, and Katsu will work steadily, muttering in Japanese to his assistant, and his wife will pour green tea and sake for the both of us all the while. Katsu's wife is beautiful, but I will not tell her that because God is there, not saying much. I will want to hear his voice, every cadence and tin can shoestring sound, but I will not know the right questions. There are too many questions, and God is hungry. And Katsu will reach over the counter with small rectangular plates for each of us, six pieces of sushi in a neat row. They will glisten, soft and bright and colorful, with gold flakes sprinkled on each one. The waiter will breeze by to explain each of the pieces, how the soft-shell shrimp is to be eaten— watch me first pinch off the head and legs, but all of it can be eaten—how the raw oyster came from Seattle, how the cod came from Maine, and whatever and whatever, and I will be happy thinking about God thinking about sushi with gold flakes. God and I will set aside the unwieldy chopsticks, pinch up the sushi in our fingers, and let each piece sit in our mouths. All of it will be exquisite, sliding down our throats splendidly. Katsu will ask how the sushi is, and God will smile, patting His stomach. And that is all this world needs. I will pretend to barter with God, trying not to let Him pay when He does not offer to, and it will be a grand fortune, but I will not mind. I will tip generously. I will order another round of sake. God will take small sips. I will tell Katsu his wife is beautiful, and I will never go home again, and God will forgive me. God will forgive me for everything. God will forgive me for not shaking His hand, or even lifting my head, and saying, "All is well!"

Donation

COURTNEY CRAGGETT

BODY TURNED TO BREAD, BLOOD to wine. Broken, poured, consumed. Wafer placed on tongue, cup tilted to mouth. Ash smeared. Fingers raised to forehead, chest, shoulders, lips. Dust to dust. Life to death to life again.

She sees it written on the back of a pickup: Wife needs kidney. Mother of three. Blood type O. The traffic is still, the sunshine thick. She feels her kidneys heavy inside her, feels them purifying, filtering. She's always been interested in something like that, the giving of one life for another—a type of motherhood, or salvation. There's a number to call on the back of the truck, and she writes it down. She learns it's an easy thing to give away a kidney. The body hardly misses it at all. The mother she saves sends her pictures of the children through the years, birthdays and Christmases and graduations. "Thank you," the mother scribbles on the back.

When donated, if only donated in part, the liver will grow back, regain full function. There is a boy who needs hers, a little boy with curly hair and big eyes, who loves everyone without trying, who saves up his quarters to give to the homeless, feeds feral cats his leftover lunch on the way home from school. She sees his picture on the evening news, and she puts her hand under her right breast, where beneath her rib cage her liver breaks down insulin, stores the vitamins that give her energy, metabolizes toxins. She thinks of the poison piling up inside the little boy's body. She schedules the surgery.

She hates the word "hero" more than any other word. People remind her of the two lives she's saved. They tell her story with cocktails in hand, her sacrifice a party trick. They don't know what she has always known, that her body aches to be poured out, given away. That she can feel each of her organs inside her individually, full of life that could save others, and she longs to be rid of them. Her sacrifice is necessary, not heroic. If she could, she'd chop off her arms and legs, dig her eyes from their sockets, knock her teeth loose and wear dentures instead. She cuts off her hair for cancer patients. It grows back, so she makes the donation recurring. She visits blood booths weekly, offers her bone marrow and plasma. She takes iron pills, eats big red steaks and piles of spinach. The doctors say her blood is the richest they've seen, that it will save many lives.

There are ways to make oneself important, ways to change the world with passion and hard work. Some people serve in soup kitchens, cook food and wash dishes and hug strangers, and some raise children, teach them right from wrong, give them the education they need for success. Some move abroad. They build health clinics or dig wells or plant gardens. But she wants something that will cost her more than that. Something she can't have back.

A man writes asking for a lung. His letter is a prayer that lists the reasons he deserves to live, the recipient both his judge and savior. She loves to run. Her lungs have carried her to marathon finish lines, have pushed her over mountain trails when her feet have long wanted to quit. Her donated liver grew back, and her single kidney does the work of two, and the cells in her blood multiply and divide and replace, but with only one lung, she will gasp for breath the rest of her life, run slow little circles around the schoolyard track, content herself with participant medals. For the first time, she wants to tell the man no, her lung is hers to keep. But is a sacrifice that costs nothing truly a sacrifice? For the first time, she feels heroic.

The donations are easy after that, and fast, one after the other. She gives away her intestines and pancreas. She gives her skin, her bones, her stem cells, one of her corneas. Everything that can grow back. Everything she can do without. Her body spreads to others, goes into the world. More of it exists outside herself than within, and she likes to think of the life that was once her own, becoming new life, falling in love, raising children, burying grandparents, traveling to Paris and Cairo and Rome.

Her heart is the last to go. She has given everything else away but wants to give more. Besides, she is tired of it, the way it swells and falls, feels too much or not enough. It can do better work in a body that is whole. "Do you want to listen one last time?" the doctor asks before he takes it, and she holds the stethoscope to her chest, feels the cold against her many scars, listens to the heartbeats that kept her alive.

When she was a child she prayed to become a martyr, one for whom the world was not worthy. Her life was never taken from her, though, and so she will give it freely. There is no greater love than this.

The doctor places the mask over Janey's mouth. He tells her to think of something happy, to count backward from ten. She closes her eyes and begins:

Ten. Nine. Eight.

She thinks of confession and absolution, baptism and rebirth. Remember that you are dust, and to dust you will return.

Seven. Six.

She feels the blood and nails in her wrists, the thorns in her forehead, the water in her side, the surge of love for this world and all who live in it.

Five. Four. Three.

Children sneak to the table and swallow the last drops of wine, stuff wafers into their mouths. Mice eat the crumbs. They carry the host away, the body and blood of our Lord spread throughout alleyways and sewers, across forests and fields.

We Don't Live by the Sea Anymore

DEANIE VALLONE

MY FIRST SIGN IS THIS: the sound of water rushing into the upstairs bath.

Growing up, Mariah lived by the sea. We both did. Four blocks away from each other on the same hangnail of land. The kind of landscape with rusted edges that fall away into the water, ports filled with wretched boats helmed by wretched men elbowing one another for room, mainland thick with neon beer signs and the reek of fish and brine and piss. Even now its ghost clings to us like a stench.

While I don't miss the town, I do miss the water. It's quieter inland, in the fields and woods that line the expanse around our house. When I was a teenager, I used to slip out of bed, out of the house, out of my clothes, stumble through the green-black of our pitiful yard to the water near our doorstep. I know what people would say: *Weren't you afraid of what lurks below?* No—I longed for something such as that. Into the cold lap of the water I would thrust myself. I would turn my face and lie on my back. The waves rocked me, settling me down, sucking at my body until I slipped into a steady buoyancy. True rest: even Mariah would appreciate that.

I sometimes wonder what Mariah would do if I did that now—sneak out of the house to go to the sea. Would she run her long hands across my cold, smooth absence? Would she pull herself awake, lean on her elbow, call my name into the blink of darkness? Would she turn herself out of bed, walk the hardwood floor barefoot, led only by outstretched fingertips? Would she know to go to the water?

When people ask how Mariah and I met, we tell them that we grew up together, which is the truth, but slanted. Because in truth, it was Brother, but we don't talk about him to each other, not anymore. In those early courtship days, our memories of him brought us together. But we were young, and the young have the luxury of opening up wounds for others to peer inside.

Out on the water I could forget. Forget what happened at school, what was said at the dinner table, what my future didn't hold, what my father didn't want me to be. I could forget me. I drew to the divide where I could be broken down into separate molecules: water, salt; then, hydrogen, oxygen. A world in circles and hexagons. I saw that painful geometry in my head, then drew the shapes in the sand, then doodled on napkins and notebook corners, then carved into my skin with a thin blade, then painted on canvases for thousands of dollars, then traced on the small of Mariah's back, the inside of her thigh. How simple life was in those moments of suspension. Letting myself descend under the surface to the point where Brother touched my heel, called me by my true name. It would be many more years before I looked him in the face.

Mariah saw Brother's face when she was ten years old. Her mother had died two weeks earlier; it was just her and her wrecked father, and it was a bad night. She only saw Brother that once, but for years later she thought she felt his presence, the way the atmosphere changes when a hurricane touches down, making the baby-fine hairs on your arms stand up. I heard somewhere that Brother looks different to every person, but I've never asked Mariah what she saw that day, twenty-odd years ago. I have not seen much of Brother in decades, but sometimes I will catch a glimpse of him, nearby, standing at the edge of the living room doorway, hovering by the oranges in the grocery store. It's like a contact that has moved too far over my pupil; I blink it straight, and he's gone.

We grew up; we moved to a fifty-acre farmhouse in the woods. Mariah loves to garden. She channels her anger and fear and hopes into the soil, watering them with salt water, if necessary. She savors the solidity. We are content out here, but we are not always happy. We are, after all, people aged in brine. For every night with wine by the fireplace or mornings twined in bed, there are those with slammed doors and her furiously digging a spade into the backyard. I think of Brother in those times. Those encapsulated nights on the water, Brother coming to me, his body both solid and weightless, a jellyfish pulsating below me in the abyss. I know Mariah would describe him as a shark, *a lurking thing*, vulgar language. I don't blame her; we fear that which we don't understand, and she cannot help but see a predator. Fear brought him to her; it clouds her. But when I called Brother, he simply slipped his hand into mine, and I know this: that some sharks can live up to 150 years, that some can glow in the dark, that they never run out of teeth, that they have remained unchanged for hundreds of millions of years.

The air inland does not smell cold or warm, sharp or grainy, wet or rotting. Its smell simply is not. Mariah has not seemed to notice, but I have. Smell is our strongest memory sense; living here dislocates me out of time and place. I wake up some mornings and wonder whether I have ceased to exist. The house we live in is perfectly polished wood and banisters, big windows and open spaces. My paintings fill the walls. There are no mementos. We don't talk about the past, and Mariah doesn't like traveling anymore, doesn't like the sea anymore, doesn't like the nickname Mary anymore. Her father's voice, slick with scotch and malice and oh so much grief, *Mary, Mary, quite contrary.*

She still likes gardens. Like my art, it allows her to make sense of herself and the world and herself in the world. Likes the visceral nature of it, the earthiness, the mathematical purity of botany. Fibonacci's spiral, she says, is why she fell in love with my paintings before she fell in love with me. Fennel, rosemary, narcissus, violet. Yellow roses, everywhere, the petals opening outward exponentially. We don't cut them and bring them into the house; she doesn't like to watch them brown and wither.

Mariah doesn't laugh a lot, but when she does it sounds like something out of a Greek myth: a brook bubbling, chimes catching the wind, a nymph's harp. It's incredible how a sound can bring you decades back in time. I can see the ten year old inside—Mariah, who was at that point still a child: chasing the dog around the front porch, lining her dolls up on the window ledge with a good view of the garden, squealing in fear and curiosity when she discovers the night-crawlers in her father's tackle box. I remember seeing her father with mine, leaving before the sun had even cracked an eyelid, gathering at the docks to set out on the water. Saw him hunched over, racked at the funeral. And months later, my mother's hushed voice in the kitchen, *drinking became a . . . he's always been such a nice . . . how could he try to do that . . .*

And years and years later. Mariah's face tucked into my chest, telling me a story of a little girl, a father's maddening grief, his hand at the back of her neck, her mouth and nose filling up with water, her fingernails scraping at the bathtub's porcelain edge, and Brother, looking her straight in the face.

I cannot say why Mariah doesn't laugh. Perhaps it's just that nothing humans do surprises her anymore.

Just as I shouldn't have been surprised that she wanted, *needed* to move away from the sea. We don't choose our fears, we don't choose our names, we don't choose the face Brother takes. I wish that now, knowing what I know, I could go to the black one more time, to see what she sees. To see it as she sees it. Because for me the water is peace. There I am not a body anymore. There I do not have a name. I am the sea, and nobody owns me. Sometimes I will write those words on my inner arm with a pen, dark enough to cover up the scars I wrote there long ago, long after the sea wasn't enough, and I wanted to look Brother in the face. At night, if Mariah is feeling sentimental, she'll run her fingertips along those words and scars as if she is trying to read me in Braille. *How do you do it?* she almost didn't ask. *Vertically,* I almost didn't tell her. *Not horizontally. In the bath.*

I am the sea, and nobody owns me. Would she have liked to know those words as a child? Perhaps it would have been some comfort for her those nights she spent in the hospital, her father in the psych ward on suicide watch. Perhaps it would have eased her of the burden of carrying wretched, brackish water inside of her belly, slowly seeping into cracks and whorls I never saw, rotting her from the inside out like festering wood, so that my first sign, water running on porcelain, is already too late.

Brother closes the door, sits down on the edge of the tub.

Vacation, Thirty-Three

CADY VISHNIAC

I'M WASTED, DRIVING UP THE Siskiyous, away from the casino, in my ex-husband's Mustang GT. Wild horses on the mountains, also called mustangs, like I told my kindergarteners back in Eaton. The kids drew mustangs—Crystal even gave me her drawing—and now I'm here, night sky, Rod Stewart blasting, *drink that white rum.* Booze, like the fried chicken in the back seat, is rough on kidneys, but I drank something anyway, a mustang, made with Wild Turkey, not rum. Rod's as full of it about the rum as my ex is about everything else: *too much* for me to get cancer in the kidneys, *too much* for me to be angry. Me, the best teacher, someone who lets cars pass when I-70 gets jammed, in California driving drunk to prove my ex wrong. He believed in New Year's resolutions, power of prayer, law of attraction, that my *negative attitude* induced this unchecked multiplying of cells. Now he's *no longer attracted.* I could wreck this Mustang, my plagued body nibbled by mustangs because of the mustang I drank. *Synchronicity,* he'd call it. Here's what I hope instead: I'll loop the mountains impaired and never get breathalyzed, never crash, because most people don't. The odds are the odds. I'll go home to the kids, and get a cat or have an affair with our janitor. I didn't have to be wrong to get sick, so I don't have to be good to live a good life. We get what we deserve; it's anything.

Afterbirth

AUBREY HIRSCH

T HE FUCKED-UP THING IS THAT I can't remember which baby was which. There were just so many of them. They kept coming out, one after another. One, two, three, four, five. My wife was feverish with contractions, shaking and vomiting from the agonists and the magnesium. She was on her back in the hospital bed, and the babies were pouring out, like water, into my hands, and she pled, "No, please, not another one." She kept asking, "How many is that?" I answered her over and over again. "One," I said. Then, "Two." Then, "Three." Then I said, "Still just three," a few times in a row. When I finally said, "Five. That's all of them. All five," she fell quiet.

The doctor handed them to me, tiny, hairless things. They were the size of hamsters, and I could see all their ribs.

"Shouldn't you put them in those glass things?" I asked. We'd known our quintuplets would be early. We'd known they'd spend time in the NICU. But we'd thought we had months yet before we met them.

"Not these babies," the doctor said. "Not at twenty-one weeks. Maybe at twenty-five weeks."

"They're going to die?" I asked. I had three of them in my hands. A nurse was wrapping the other two in blankets: one blue, one pink. "For sure? All of them?"

The doctor gave me a look that said, "For sure. All of them."

When he left, we took turns holding them. We shifted them around between us as we named them. We hadn't decided on any names. It was a big job, and we'd thought we had time. But now the names came easily from our lips. "Jamie." "Sandy." "Peter." There was nothing to argue over: no playground bullying in their futures, no introductions to be made. "Alice." "Joseph."

Some of the babies were dead already when we were passing them back and forth. The others died, one by one. They were so small; we couldn't really tell when it happened. A nurse came in after an hour or so and examined them.

"They've all gone," she said, "but you can hold them as long as you want to."

Knowing they were dead made me not want to touch them, but my wife went on nuzzling them and kissing their tiny, transparent faces. I wanted to say goodbye. I wanted to call them each by name, but we'd scrambled them up so effectively, I didn't know who was who. I didn't know which one had opened his eyes to look at me for a moment, which had breathed, feebly, in my arms, and which had been corpses from the start. It was a terrible feeling, not to know my own children.

My wife has healed physically. And emotionally, better than I. She says she felt she expelled some of the sadness with the afterbirth. She could feel it coming out of her like cotton, like barbed wire, like ashes, like snow.

But me? I still carry it with me. It is real and deep, and I want it to break inside me like a fever. I want to expel it now while it is still young, while it will still die. I can see all of their faces. Some are dead. Some are sleeping. They all look the same. I repeat their names over and over to myself like a prayer: JamieSandyPeterAliceJoseph JamieSandyPeterAliceJoseph JamieSandyPeterAliceJoseph JamieSandyPeterAliceJoseph.

interviews

A Conversation with Emily St. John Mandel

ASHLEY PETRY

Emily St. John Mandel is the bestselling author of Station Eleven, *a post-apocalyptic novel told from the perspective of a traveling Shakespeare troupe. It won the 2015 Arthur C. Clarke Award, appeared on multiple "best books of the year" lists, and was a finalist for the National Book Award and the PEN/Faulkner Award. It was also, her website states, "by all accounts kind of an unsettling read on an airplane."*

In addition, Mandel is the author of three previous novels: Last Night in Montreal, The Lola Quartet, *and* The Singer's Gun. *The latter won the 2014 Prix Mystère de la Critique in France. Her short fiction and essays have appeared in numerous anthologies, such as* The Best American Mystery Stories 2013 *and* Goodbye to All That: Writers on Loving and Leaving New York. *She is also a staff writer for* The Millions, *where she reviews books and makes pie charts about the trend of book titles styled as* The _____'s Daughter.

During her recent visit to Butler University as part of the Vivian S. Delbrook Visiting Writers Series, Mandel sat down with Booth *to chat about the magic of Shakespeare, the never-ending challenge of self-doubt, and the benefits of dual citizenship in uncertain political times.*

Ashley Petry I want to start by asking about your first novel, *Last Night in Montreal*. My favorite thing about that book is the discussion of vanishing languages—how every time a language dies out we lose not just the vocabulary but also whole ways of looking at the world. What got you started thinking about that?

Emily St. John Mandel I read an interesting article in *The Atlantic* by the linguist Michael Krauss. This would have been way back in 2005 or 2006. It was really my introduction to the topic. I hadn't known anything about dead and endangered languages, and sometimes you're just struck by something. I was haunted by the idea of languages disappearing, and haunted by the reality of how human it is. You tend to think of languages as these somewhat abstract, not very personal vehicles for expression, but what it inevitably comes down to is one last speaker. You know, there are ten people who speak the language, and then two, and then there's one person. I remember a quote from a woman in the piece, I can't remember what the language was, but she was the last speaker. She spoke the dominant language around her, but she said, "But I still dream in my own language, and I can't tell anybody my dreams. It's lonely being the last one." That just pierced me through. I was so struck by it. And for me, whenever I'm writing a novel, I find that my interests at the time kind of adhere themselves to the text.

AP Was there a particular linguistic way of looking at the world that really struck you?

ESM I remember being struck by the idea that there might be ideas that are very easily and naturally expressed in one language but not in another. You even see it in languages as similar as English and French. Try to come up with an English equivalent for the French *déjà vu*. Those two words sum up a feeling, a sensation, a thing that are otherwise only explainable by entire clumsy paragraphs, if at all. I was fascinated by the idea that maybe every language has an idea like that.

AP In your next novel, *The Singer's Gun*, the character Elena talks about having "a gene for escape," and I noticed that escape and travel are themes throughout your novels. Is that something you relate to personally, that need or desire for escape?

ESM Yeah, I suppose it is. You know, there was nothing wrong with my childhood. It was happy enough. But I did always want something different. And I moved to New York City eventually, via Toronto and Montreal. My whole family is still in that corner of southwestern British Columbia where I grew up, and an interesting thing about a place like New York that people tend to move to is that you encounter a lot of people with that gene for escape, where they were driven toward some other place or some other idea of a way to live. So it is something that preoccupies me. I left home when I was eighteen, and it was kind of extreme. I went from British Columbia to Toronto, which was a distance of, I don't know, two thousand miles. And it was just fascinating to me to realize that you could get on a plane and fly into an entirely different life. So I think that's an idea that I've been exploring in fiction ever since.

AP When you went to Toronto, it was to attend the School of Toronto Dance Theatre. What was that journey for you, from dance to writing?

ESM Yeah, that's a strange trajectory. I had always written as a hobby from the time I was really little, and it was never something that I took at all seriously. It was just something I did on my own time. But there was a period when I was about twenty, twenty-one, living in Montreal and dancing, when I realized I just didn't really love to dance anymore. That's a really hard life. You don't want to do it unless you love it. So I found myself thinking, *What else can I do? What comes next?* I didn't have a high school diploma, let alone a BA, and it was around that time when I realized I was pretty intensely drawn to writing, even though it wasn't something that I'd ever thought of as a career. So I started writing what eventually became my first novel, *Last Night in Montreal.* So for me it was just a very gradual transition of going from thinking of myself as a dancer who sometimes wrote to thinking of myself as a writer who sometimes danced.

AP Okay. One thing that struck me about *The Singer's Gun* is that, we talk about Chekhov's gun and how if you put a gun in the beginning of a story, you have to use it. Well, you have it in the title, which is an extreme example of that. Why did you choose that title?

ESM It's actually a controversial title. My French publisher hates it, which is why the book is published in France as *On Ne Joue Pas Avec La Mort— One Does Not Play with Death.* Believe it or not, that works in French. It's a little melodramatic in English. And conversely, *The Singer's Gun* absolutely does not work in French. It sounds like a B movie. But in English it's fine. But, yeah, I love that title. It was partly just that I thought it sounded cool. And it was partly that, at that moment in the plot, I wanted the reader to have a little jolt. Like, "Oh, my god, there's the singer and the gun, and something is going to happen." So it was useful in terms of developing tension at that moment in the plot.

AP Elsewhere in that novel you quote "Air and Light and Time and Space," the Charles Bukowski poem about how if you're going to create, you're going to do it "even with a cat crawling up your back while the whole city trembles." Is that what the act of creation is like for you?

ESM Not really. I mean, I am absolutely drawn to writing in what you could describe as a compulsive way. I'll write on Starbucks napkins if I don't have any paper with me. But I would not actually write with a cat . . . how does a person even do that? I don't have a ton of admiration for Bukowski, for his poetry, although I do love his screenplays. But I thought that was a funny line and a funny idea in that moment for somebody who was maybe taking writing too seriously.

AP I was tempted, thinking about the questions I wanted to ask you, to say, has this process of creation changed for you since you became a mother? And then I thought, you know, I don't think I would ask that question of a male writer.

ESM Oh, that's interesting.

AP So I think it's an inherently sexist question, and I'm not going to ask it. But it made me think to ask, are you encountering those kinds of sexist questions and expectations as you travel for book tours?

ESM I am, yes. You're right. And that is the kind of question that male writers don't get asked. At the same time, there are very practical logistical differences in writing with a child versus not writing with a child that probably male writers would run into anyway, just in terms of timing and childcare. I feel incredibly fortunate in that I have childcare six hours a day, Monday through Friday, and that makes it possible. But I guess I would have to think about male writers on an individual basis, to think about how applicable that is to their lives, because of course there is still this expectation, even in 2017, that taking care of the child is the woman's job. That's just kind of the default.

AP Sure. So I read *The Lola Quartet* recently, and it struck me—well, this strikes me in all of your books—that they have such a complex structure, with multiple POVs and various timelines. Writing the books, how do you manage all of that?

ESM I probably keep it less straight than one might imagine from reading the final product. I end up with incredibly incoherent first drafts. The first draft was just a train wreck, really for all four of the books. And for me it's really in the revisions that it all comes together, that you get any kind of clarity or cohesion that exists. So I write an incoherent first draft, and then I revise it a hundred times until it's readable.

AP That sounds painful.

ESM It can be painful, but I actually prefer the revision to trying to figure out what comes next. It's easier for me, to be honest. Maybe it's different for everybody. But I feel like, if I have something, anything, no matter how rough it is, I can make it better, whereas trying to figure out what that thing is, to me that's the hard part and the scary part and the part where I feel like I don't know what I'm doing. There's something satisfying in feeling like I have the thing and I just need to refine it.

AP What's been the biggest challenge you've faced during that process? Was it a particular book, a particular scene?

ESM That's a good question. In *Station Eleven*, the hardest scene to write was the prophet's death, just trying to strike a balance between making it a big enough moment in the plot but not wanting to go all slow-motion Hollywood explosions. I must have rewritten that scene ten times, and it was really hard to strike the right balance in that moment of climax.

The hardest thing for me generally in writing is doubt, which is probably true for a lot of writers. And it's interesting to me that that never really leaves you. You know, I'm working on my fifth novel, and I still have those moments when I feel like I don't know what I'm doing. So the moral of the story is that doubt is always with you, and you have to be willing to live with it.

AP Okay, let's talk about *Station Eleven*, since you mentioned it. First of all, what motivated you to focus on a time period twenty years after the apocalypse, which offers up a different kind of drama?

ESM That was a very deliberate decision on my part. It seemed to me that most of the post-apocalyptic and dystopian novels that I'd read and most of the films that I'd seen had been set in that territory immediately following the complete societal breakdown, where it's all horror and mayhem and chaos. And I think that that period would absolutely occur, but it's just not plausible to me that it would last forever, at least not everywhere on Earth. So it was more interesting to me to write about what comes next, what's the new world and the new culture that begins to emerge fifteen or twenty years down the line. So it was partly just personal interest; partly not wanting to write a horror novel, just as a matter of personal preference; and partly feeling that that horrific ground had been so well covered by other writers.

AP So why tell the story through the lens of this traveling Shakespeare troupe?

ESM They were actually the original idea for the story. Originally *Station Eleven* was going to be set in present-day Canada, and it was always going to be about the lives of people in a traveling Shakespearean theater company. I don't know, maybe that would have been a good book, but it seems kind of boring when I think about it now. I wanted to write about the technology that surrounds us, and it seemed to me that an interesting way to write about that would be to think about its absence. So I decided to keep that original idea of the traveling players but place them in a post-apocalyptic landscape. And it was an interesting contrast, having these things that we think of as being very refined expressions of civilization, like symphonies and plays, occurring in this kind of wild landscape.

AP Without the apocalypse it would have been like *Slings and Arrows*.

ESM Yeah, which I didn't see until after I finished it, but I love that show. It's so good.

AP This leads me into my next question, which is that I'm a huge Shakespeare fan, and *King Lear* is my personal favorite.

ESM Same here. That probably says something terrible about us, but it's so good.

AP It is. So I loved seeing Lear's story woven into the novel, but tell me why you chose to focus on that particular play. Besides it being your favorite, were there thematic things that you were also interested in pulling in?

ESM There were a few reasons. One had to do with the character in question, Arthur Leander. He just struck me as the kind of actor who waits all his life to be old enough to play King Lear. You know, that's *the* part for older male actors. So it was very fitting with his character.

Also, I liked the idea of echoing some of the themes of *Lear* throughout the larger novel. Lear loses three daughters; Arthur loses three wives. There's a similar dynamic at play of becoming removed from the world—either removed by power, I suppose, in Lear's case or by fame in Arthur's case. These are distancing things. And about regret and loss later in life.

It also had to do with the moment in the plot when the play appears, that it's performed on a night when this devastating flu pandemic has just arrived in Toronto. And of course on one level *Lear* is a play about losing absolutely everything, and that's the situation of everybody in the theater that night. They're kind of suspended in this last moment of the normal world. They're just on the verge of losing absolutely everything.

AP One of my favorite books as a kid was *The Green Book* by Jill Paton Walsh, and part of the premise is that people have to flee Earth on a spaceship and can bring only one book each to the new planet. It broke my heart because they didn't have time to coordinate, so they ended up with three copies of *Robinson Crusoe* but no Shakespeare.

ESM Oh, no. Tragedy.

AP Exactly. So is *King Lear* the play you would take in that context? I ask because it's possible to choose *Lear* as your personal favorite while also acknowledging that a different play is better or more important.

ESM That's a great question. I think I would still take *Lear*. It's a terrible basis for a new civilization on an alien planet. It's really dark. But there's just so much in there. There's such a richness in that play.

AP What got you interested in Shakespeare to begin with?

ESM I just saw a few productions and loved them. And particularly a production that I saw in New York City in 2006. The director was James Lapine, and King Lear was Kevin Kline, and it was just a spectacular production. It was so moving to me. Even the staging was incredibly moving. He had the three little girls on stage playing childhood versions of Lear's daughters, so I borrowed that staging in the book because I was so moved by it.

AP Okay, let's switch gears. Somebody asked you in an interview several years ago about the Museum of Civilization that is created in *Station Eleven*—about what object you would place into it if you were going to do that. You said a globe. Is that still what you would choose?

ESM Yeah, it is. I think it would be so easy to lose sight of the larger world. You know, I think about how local your world would become, and how you wouldn't know what was happening in Denver, let alone China. And it would be really possible to forget that the world was that big. So I think to maintain perspective a globe would be a useful thing.

AP Which makes sense if you have a gene for escape.

ESM Yeah, exactly. You want to map out where you would have gone if the world hadn't ended.

AP My writer friends and I often joke that we would be completely useless during the apocalypse because we have no practical skills.

ESM I would be useless.

AP Well, that's my question. Do you have any apocalypse skills? Do you secretly know how to weld?

ESM No, I don't. I don't even remember how to fish, and I grew up in British Columbia. I've been fishing. But I would be useless. I've told a couple of people that they could join my traveling Shakespearean theater company, though. Maybe we'll pick up stragglers as we go.

AP Do you play an instrument?

ESM The most useless instrument. I play the piano. I mean, nobody is hauling a piano on that caravan.

AP So I noticed that the "About" section of your website says, "St. John is my middle name. File the books under M." That's kind of an unusual middle name. Is there a backstory?

ESM There is. I had an incredibly British great-grandfather, Newell St. Andrew St. John, which is the most British name in the history of names. That's peak UK. So my grandmother was Ella St. John. She was somebody who traveled the world and loved books and was friends with Alice Munro. I've always wished I could meet Alice Munro and ask, "Do you remember my grandmother?" And my mother wanted to keep the name in the family, so my middle name is St. John after that side of the family. But it makes for such a confusing name, so my books are under S half the time and Mandel half the time, and half the reviews will refer to me as Ms. St. John Mandel. But it's my daughter's middle name, as well. I like the idea of carrying these names forward through time.

AP Speaking of your daughter, last spring you published an article in *Humanities* where you talked about being pregnant, watching news coverage of all the mass shootings, and wondering whether the United States was still the right place to raise your child. And you write to your future daughter, "We'll try to protect you in this terrifying country." It strikes me that the United States at the moment is more terrifying than ever, so I'm wondering if this is still a question you're asking yourself.

ESM Very much so. It's a complicated question. I mean, I grew up in Canada, and, if we're to be honest, if you're raised in a leftwing family in Canada, which I was, that's a very anti-American environment, even though my father was from the United States. So I always had a reflexive aversion to the US. But then I fell in love with New York City and realized how incredibly provincial it is to think about any national group in those enormous general terms. These are the revelations you have when you're twenty-one.

I guess I was a little bit surprised by how much I cared about the most recent election. I hadn't realized how invested in this country I was, but I really did care. And it is a question that's very much on my mind. During that period when I was writing that essay and traveling a lot, there were an incredible number of mass shootings that year, and it got to the point where I found myself thinking, as a parent, is it irresponsible of me to raise a child in this country? Of course there's no such thing as the perfect country, and obviously anyone is more likely to be hit by a car than to be involved in a massacre, but at the same time, there'd be story after story, and I'd just think, God, there's no way she's going to school here. So that was very much on my mind.

I think what kind of country we become is very much an open question. I don't know what it will look like after this administration, if it will be a good place to live in, say, twenty or thirty years. My daughter has dual citizenship because I was born Canadian with dual citizenship, as well, and there is something reassuring to me in that. Not to say that Canada couldn't be prey to the same nationalist, populist instincts. It's absolutely possible that it could happen there too. But it's nice to think that she has options, that she could live elsewhere legally if things went drastically wrong on this side of the border.

AP How do you think a writer can respond to what we see happening in the country right now?

ESM I don't know. I think a big part of it has to do with keeping hold of the idea that this isn't normal, and keeping hold of the idea that there is something fundamentally anti-American, in terms of the project of this country and its founding principles, in rejecting people from a particular religion. That's not patriotism. That's anti-Americanism. It's against everything we stand for. I think a lot of the responsibilities that writers have are the same as the responsibilities that one has as a citizen, which is not letting this become normalized, not being silent when appalling things are happening. These are such strange times to navigate.

AP Absolutely. You said you fell in love with New York. What about it?

ESM Just its kind of electric quality. There's a book I really love by Rem Koolhaas called *Delirious New York,* and he talks about a culture of congestion. We tend to think of too many people being crammed together as automatically a bad thing, but his argument was that too many people crammed together can create this heightened environment that's kind of exciting. You can feel this friction. There are parts of New York that bother me, but there is a kind of electrical charge to it, even now, and I've been there thirteen years. And there's a culture of work there that I really like. It can obviously go wrong really quickly—there are people who just work themselves to the bone. But it's a city whose overarching culture is that you work very hard, long hours, and I like that culture. I like the discipline of it, if it's work that you love.

AP So what are you reading?

ESM I just finished *Another Brooklyn* by Jacqueline Woodson, and I loved it. She has the most clear, lucid prose style. It's the kind of prose that almost seems simple when you're reading it, but you have to be a writer to realize how difficult that is, to make it look easy. I really admired that book. I thought it was wonderful.

AP I know you get some of the same questions over and over again. Is there a particular question that you're just tired of answering? It's okay if I asked it.

ESM Yes. I hate it when people say, "Where do you get your ideas?" I just don't know.

AP Just out of the ether.

ESM Yeah, I don't know how that works, so I never have a good answer for that one.

AP Okay. Is there anything I haven't asked you, that you wish people knew about you or your work?

ESM I just like to emphasize that *Station Eleven* isn't a horror novel, because I think people see the post-apocalyptic label and they think of cannibalism.

AP No cannibalism. Check. For certain characters, there are time periods immediately after the flu that you gloss over. You don't really give us the details of the horrible things that happen to them during that time. Do you know what those horrible things are, or did you just try not to dwell on it too much?

ESM It's case by case. I don't know what happened to Kiersten in that year on the road that I don't dwell on. But I did write a chapter about Tyler's childhood from the time he leaves the airport, and that was really gratuitously horrific, so I ended up cutting it. I felt like I didn't need it. Sometimes a suggestion of horror is as effective as spelling out the blood spatters on the page.

A Conversation with Joyce Carol Oates

SUSAN LERNER

In the Kenyon Review, *Joyce Carol Oates once wrote, "Writing is our way of assuaging homesickness," and this is the quote that came to mind in the fall of 2015 when Oates read as part of Butler University's Vivian S. Delbrook Visiting Writers Series. At Clowes Hall, she read from her memoir* The Lost Landscape: A Writer's Coming of Age, *which tells of her childhood home and her formative years. She read with ease, pausing occasionally with a humorous aside. Oates, the serious-looking woman on the book jackets of countless dark novels, is funny.*

In the introduction to The Best American Essays of the Century, *an anthology Oates edited, she wrote: "Art should provoke, disturb, arouse our emotions, expand our sympathies in directions we may not anticipate and may not even wish." Oates carries this sentiment through in her novels and stories, which provoke and disturb by employing plots that often spark from an act of violence. The author's empathetic prose never excuses her characters' cruelty, but informs it by providing a window into their deepest hurts and desires.*

Oates's list of accomplishments, still growing after fifty years in the field, is so vast and unwieldy that it defies attempts to catalogue. Her work ethic embodies the historically American idea of success—a Horatio Alger story—that a dream can be achieved through perseverance and hard work. But Oates's career also fits another narrative of success, that some individuals are born with a bounteous talent. In The Lost Landscape, *Oates reveals that as a girl she told stories by coloring pictures with her Crayolas because her desire to narrate came before she learned to write. Oates's oeuvre fills bookshelves and includes novels, short story collections, memoirs, essays, and literary criticism. The* New York Times *has included dozens of her books on its list of notable books of the year, and other honors include the National Book Award, nominations for the Pulitzer Prize, the National Humanities Medal bestowed by former president Barack Obama, and the PEN Center USA Award for Lifetime Achievement.*

After her reading, Oates fielded questions from the audience, and the next morning she sat in a room with thirty students to answer more questions. In this more casual setting she spoke about being a formalist. She explained that different stories call out for specific types of language, and that she is always seeking forms to tell the multitude of stories that crowd her head and fill her files at home. "I'm really happy when I'm running," she said. "I get lots of ideas when I run." Before Oates headed home she sat down with Booth.

Susan Lerner You're best known as a fiction writer, but you have recently penned two memoirs: *A Widow's Story* and *The Lost Landscape.* Some reviewers of *The Lost Landscape* have commented that they've sensed a reticence or guardedness in your autobiographical writing, and one review included your quote: "Nothing is more offensive than an adult child exposing his or her elderly parents to the appalled fascination of strangers." Confessional memoir has become so popular that it has recently been coined "The First-Person Industrial Complex." What are your feelings about confessional writing?

Joyce Carol Oates There are many degrees of confessional writing. I think that if one feels a compulsion to confess in great detail, particularly medical features of one's life, I don't understand why one would feel that way, but I wouldn't say that you shouldn't do it. I would say that one might think twice about revealing medical details about one's parents. Confession is one thing, and I don't really think it's a good idea, but to confess for other people, it is really morally questionable.

SL Even if facts about other people impact your own life?

JCO Everything impacts everything. We have digestive problems some-times. Do we need to write about that? We live in physical bodies. It's not necessary that we have to detail everything. Some of us go to the dentist. We have our teeth cleaned. That may impact your life for a day, but do you need to write about that? Something like that is not that significant. Look, everybody dies. Everybody has parents who get elderly and die. Do we really need to know aesthetic, excruciating details of each case? I don't think so. It's not illuminating. It's sort of morbid and meretricious.

SL In *The Lost Landscape* you wrote that as a child you understood books to belong to one of two categories: books for children and books for adults. Literature for young adults does venture into more sophisticated themes these days, and many adult fans of young adult books claim that this genre travels the same emotional territory as literature for adults. Others insist that fiction written for adults provides a more enriching reading expe-rience. I'm curious, because you've written both young adult and adult fiction, what your thoughts are.

JCO You just quoted me. What exactly is the question? My thoughts on young adult writing?

SL My question was whether you thought that books for young adults—for instance, I loved *After the Wreck, I Picked Myself Up, Spread My Wings, and Flew Away*—if you feel as though adults who are fans of YA literature can get the same kind of enriching literary experience as by reading adult literature.

JCO I'm not sure that's a question. I don't understand. Yeah, that sounds like a good idea. Possibly people are reading young adult fiction because the vocabulary is simpler. They're easier to read. They're much easier to read than Virginia Woolf, or James Joyce, or Faulkner. So they're read-ing young adult fiction because it's easier to read. *Huckleberry Finn*, you could say, is young adult fiction. *To Kill a Mockingbird* is young adult, [as is] *Catcher in the Rye*. There are young adult books of fiction that are quite relevant. *Huckleberry Finn* is a great classic. There's nothing wrong with reading it. I think that's why they're reading it—it's easier to read.

SL   In 2012, when Philip Roth retired, the *New York Times* quoted him: "I knew I wasn't going to get another good idea, or if I did I'd have to slave over it. Writing is frustration—it's daily frustration, not to mention humiliation." How do you feel about the writing process?

JCO   I know Philip. He's a friend of mine. Philip's attitude toward writing is different from my own. It was much more grim and difficult for him. He wasn't happy with his last several books. They're very short books, short novels. He also had health problems. He had a quadruple bypass, and he has had other problems, so I think physically—he was eighty-something—all that's part of it. I don't think he would have written that or said those things when he was forty years old.

SL   In *The Lost Landscape* you wrote about your love of literary journals. Bill Henderson, the publisher and editor of the Pushcart Prize, wrote in 2012 that "instant internet publication is damaging to writers." As a cofounder of the *Ontario Review,* what are your thoughts concerning the legitimacy of online literary journals?

JCO   Oh, I think they're fine. I don't have any strong feeling. *Narrative Magazine* is online, and it's quite excellent. I think what Bill Henderson meant was that probably the writers were not being edited, so that there's a lot of, evidently, unedited work. I think it's pretty harmless.

SL I have a question about the dustup last year with the white male poet who used the Chinese pseudonym. How do you feel about this as a road to publication?

JCO I don't have any strong feelings about it. I don't know why people have to have strong feelings. Everybody gets angry about things, and lots of them got angry with him. Obviously as a poet he would have preferred being published under his own name. He is a serious poet. He got more easily published under this other name that turned out to be somebody's name from his high school. He just had some bad luck. Rather than just see it as a kind of farcical thing, people seem to be really attacking him and choosing to be really unhappy about it.

SL In Meg Wolitzer's piece for the *New York Times Sunday Book Review* in 2012 titled "The Second Shelf," she wrote that much literary fiction written by women is relegated to a lower tier, a category labeled "women's fiction," while the top shelf is reserved for books of prominence, which are, for the most part, written by men. What are your thoughts on "the second shelf"?

JCO I'm not so much aware of it. I'm sure it may be true.

SL I wonder if that might be because you've reached a stature at which you're less aware, maybe, of women who haven't quite made a name for themselves?

JCO There are many, many, many men who don't even get published, and a lot of them, too, are on the second or third tier, but nobody knows their names. There are a whole lot of mid-list writers, and I do know a lot of male writers who don't do very well. Women writers have more of a built-in audience. Jennifer Weiner docs complain about not being considered on the same shelf with Jonathan Franzen, but she has a very wide readership. A male writer of her stature or quality or subject matter would not have those readers.

SL Jennifer Weiner—

JCO She's a former student of mine.

SL Jennifer Weiner came out in support of women who write all over the gamut of literary arts. She lamented about the solidarity, or the lack of solidarity, amongst women writers. She said that male literary writers, for the most part, don't object to the meager coverage of male genre writers, whereas female literary writers react badly to any coverage of female genre writers, horrified that this might take attention away from them. What—

JCO Who's horrified? Where's this coming from?

SL That's something she said.

JCO Horrified? I can't think of one person who's horrified by any of that. I mean, I really don't know what she's talking about. Maybe some friends of hers in Brooklyn, or wherever she lives. Basically, I have no idea what she's talking about.

SL You don't sense a lack of solidarity among women writers?

JCO I don't know what kind of an issue it is. What she means . . . I have no idea what she's talking about. She wants more attention for her books. You know, many people do. Many people want more attention for their books—and she's one of them. But she does make a lot of money; she's an enormous bestseller. Jodi Picoult, another Princeton student, sells millions of copies of her books. There are many male writers who sell a fraction. They may have better literary reputations than the women writers, but that doesn't really transfer into anything real. It's hard to have both. You could have a large readership, like *Fifty Shades of Grey,* and probably the common denominator readership is fairly low. You're not going to have a huge readership for Faulkner, because it's difficult. So if Jennifer Weiner wants a large readership, she can't also have an elite reputation. Basically, you can't really do both. There are some good writers like Toni Morrison who have a wide readership, but nothing like *Fifty Shades of Grey.* If you want enormous bestsellers, you can't write difficult novels, and probably they're not going to have difficult literary themes. So basically, you can't do both.

SL   Let's get back to your memoir *The Lost Landscape.* I've thought about the passage in which you wrote that the childhood scenes required some invention. In that ongoing debate about truth in memoir, the James Frey issue—

JCO   Right, but he didn't say that and he didn't have an afterword. I put it in an afterword, so I said it. I'm making it very clear that these are composite figures and I invented things, so if somebody is upset by that, they shouldn't read the book! With James Frey I think it was the idea that it was true. But probably, if he had to do it over again, he'd have an afterword. James Frey had written a novel, it was basically a novel, and his editor said, "No, we'd rather have it as a memoir." He was a young writer, and he was sort of tempted. I won't say he was coerced, but he wouldn't have done that on his own. He had written a novel. And then it was published as a memoir, and it was attacked for having fictitious elements.

SL   So when I ask you what measure of fact a memoir writer owes readers, your answer to that is . . .

JCO   It depends on who they are. How do we know whether any memoirs are true? How do we know whether biographies are true? There are a dozen biographies of Robert Frost that present the man in different ways. One of them is maybe more true than the others, but we don't know which one. Where is the truth? There are memoirs that claim that people have been reincarnated, or taken up in UFOs. There's a memoir about a boy who went to heaven and came back. They're all different. Readers can sort of make judgments for themselves. I like Mary Karr's writing very much, and I assume that she has to be inventing some of the dialogue that took place fifty years ago because nobody could remember that. But I think she's pretty truthful in talking about the memoir, using elements of fiction and trying to be truthful to the essence. If there was a girl in your high school to whom something awful happened, you could write about that without giving her name and her address and everything about her. You could write about the circumstances without revealing the person.

A Conversation with Brenda Shaughnessy

NATALIE LOUISE TOMBASCO

Brenda Shaughnessy's books include So Much Synth *(Copper Canyon Press, 2016) and* Our Andromeda *(Copper Canyon Press, 2012). She is a recipient of the James Laughlin Award from the Academy of American Poets and the Guggenheim Fellowship for Creative Arts. She has taught at Columbia University, the New School, Princeton University, and New York University, and she is currently an assistant professor of English at Rutgers University, where she also teaches in the MFA program. She lives in New Jersey with her family.*

 Shaughnessy visited Butler University as part of the Vivian S. Delbrook Visiting Writers Series in fall 2016, offering a soft-spoken invitation into her bitingly honest odes of girlhood. Later Shaughnessy sat down with Booth *to discuss her latest collection, which Ada Limón described as "a brilliant feminist excavation of adolescence," as well as mold-breaking, her poetic toolbox, rape culture, and being a "nasty woman."*

Natalie Louise Tombasco In your latest collection, *So Much Synth*, synthetization is at the forefront—this idea of combining multiple elements, such as past and future, through music, specifically the "zingy computer music" of the 1980s. Artists such as the Smiths, Dead or Alive, and Culture Club create this electric pulse through the pages, a soundtrack for the coming-of-age narrative. I found the musical accompaniment enjoyable because it encouraged me to revel in the speaker's nostalgia. Some writers avoid placing a Chevy, for example, in a poem for fear that it may diminish its timelessness. Was the use of cultural references ever a concern? And what do you think is the value of their presence?

Brenda Shaughnessy Well, it was definitely deliberate. I mean, I suddenly understood that whatever music you loved best when you were thirteen or fourteen is just forever indelibly imprinted on your soul, and you'll always kind of think it's the best thing in the world—because it made you, because it happened at the exact moment when your desire was being formed. And so music is always a safe place to put that desire. You fall in love with whatever band, fantasize about whoever you love in that band, and it's safe—you don't have to do anything—and you can go kind of wild. This is one of the first ways that we experiment with what we actually want. Not what somebody else thinks we want, and not what somebody else puts on us, but what we actually choose. The first time you do that is very, very powerful.

For me, it was the realization that even when the music has long been understood to be the worst—synth pop for a long time was considered to be "Ughhhh! It's the worst!"—but even if it's the objective worst, you will still think it's subjectively the best, and you'll always have a soft spot for it. I also went to see Duran Duran a few years ago, and it was so weird. They're like these old guys—but they're my old guys! They just seemed like they were so the same—the sound was so exactly the same. It was nostalgia, for sure, but it was also figuring it out and claiming it. It made me think, you know, I'm not going to pretend that this was not what happened. It brought me back to those moments of pubescence and adolescence, where I realized that so much of my reality was secret.

So much coming of age happened just listening to records and externalizing that—how you create your desire system, how you create what you love and care about, how you create a passion before the world comes, crushes it, and tells you that you can't have any of these things because it'll be dictated to you. Before rape culture comes in and kind of takes away this agency. It's nostalgic, looking back, but it's also looking back with a critical eye on just how violent that passage was. You know, just out of desperate sadness that it hasn't gotten any better.

NLT The mixtape is one of these artifacts from the '80s that you describe as a "private language, lost art, / first book, cri de coeur, X-ray, diary." The production of a mixtape was a tool of communication for a generation to establish identity, create permanency, and say, "Not 'Love me!' so much as 'Listen to me! Listen to me always!'" Would you say this book is your mixtape to the reader, the beloved seeking understanding and connection? How does this mixtape idea parallel to the immortality of the poet?

BS Mortality is more like it. Those mixtape poems are an ode to a lost art. The feelings behind the art, meaning "I want you to love me," that most certainly was lost upon hand-off. The person receiving it might never have felt any of that. The fate of the eventual mixtape is that of a book. It may end up in a bookstore, in a library, on a bedside table—or it may not. It may end up never opened, never read, no one ever really cares about it—but that isn't the point. Mortality is inescapable. You can't make something that makes you immortal. But you can memorialize your love, your feelings, your way of seeing the world. You can inscribe it as best you can in something that seems at the time to be a medium that may last.

Maybe I do like that idea that it's a mixtape of a book—but there's no B-side, right? Mostly I think the music of that period allowed me to organize not only my memories, but my critical apparatus for those years, in a way that I didn't feel I had any power at that time. Now, looking back as a grown-up, it's like I can call that what that was. I have enough distance and authority over it.

NLT What do you think is the equivalent of the mixtape today?

BS Audio technology today is so fast and nonlinear. You used to have to listen to songs in order. People used to save up money to buy albums. Now you just buy songs here or there, or just steal it—or whatever people do. There is no equivalent. It's gone.

NLT   In your long poem "Is There Something I Should Know," our heroine makes the transition from innocence to experience—her sexual awakening during the seven hundred days of puberty, while Duran Duran echoes in the background. She deals with feeling "Extra Medium," the secrecy of tampons, her worth determined by fuckability, ending sentences in question marks, a constant reminder of the violence that blossoms with girlhood. As a mother of a daughter, can you speak more of your intentions with this poem and the "[un]restricted girl-version" of growing up you hope for her?

BS   Thanks for that question—that's really key for me. No one ever thinks about what would be there if the threat of violence, the objectification, or the sort of gradual and then all of a sudden humiliation and diminution of girls didn't happen. What would be in its place? So you have girls from the time they're eight years old being told "Oh, be quieter" or "You're not good enough to be on our team" or "You're a girl, you can't xyz." The gendered world does this particular violence to boys, too. Absolutely. And I think it starts earlier than puberty. However, it becomes a different thing in puberty. Girls are given the impression that they shouldn't outdo, outsmart, be stronger, louder, or anything more than boys. They're given this idea early on and consistently, from teachers, coaches, other kids, parents—everybody tells them that they should never be more than boys—and because of what? Because boys don't like it. And if boys don't like it, then they don't like you, and then what are you going to do? Not be liked by boys? That's a heavy price because boys dominate in all places and spaces.

NLT   Right. We've seen it play out in this previous election, as well, with Hillary Clinton and the "nasty woman" dig.

BS   Oh, yeah—you see it a lot in the election. I mean, I cannot count how many women I've talked to who said, "I'm crying through this whole thing," because it brings up so much. You see Hillary Clinton bullied for the way she talks, being smart and prepared—but that's how boys treat you in junior high school. You can't escape, whether you're beautiful, plain, in-between, smart, not smart, athletic—everybody gets it. They'll find something to knock you down. And it is epidemic! Then when adolescence happens it turns sexual, and you can use this vulnerability that girls have against them. Suddenly bodies become public property, and it's completely sick. What would happen if a girl wasn't told what she could or couldn't be, tone it down, be quieter, she should act more like a girl and diminish herself for her own wellbeing—for her own good? What if when she came into puberty, came into her woman body, what if it wasn't filled with shame? What if getting your period wasn't something everyone could make fun of all the time? What if this time was a sacred process that was considered beautiful, normal, and, most importantly, her body?

The permission and agency of what your body is for and what it does—that's just gone. It's taken before you even know what "consent" is. I mean, how do you know—already leered at when you were ten, commented on in your ballet outfit. It starts so young, and we're all led to believe it's just us, something's wrong with us. The foundation for sexual assault and rape has already been laid down since we were babies, so we don't know whose body it really is, and you can't ask anybody. This is a basic right. Your human, bodily autonomy. You have no agency, from the time you're little to an unwanted pregnancy. And that's just the way it is. You can't walk out on the street wearing what you want because someone's going to say something, and then you got what you deserved. What could we have done with all that energy if we didn't have to worry about all that? We would be more well-read, relaxed, and free walking out of any door—any time, day or night—free to be with our friends to learn, explore, and experiment in the world . . . which we know we cannot do now. And it's crushing, though, to know that now I have a five year old, and I had forty years to change it, and I didn't do it. We didn't change the world in time for this one little girl who I'm in charge of.

NLT So how do we change that awkwardness and secrecy in order to embrace little girls, with all their abilities and desires?

BS We break that mold. If those secretive qualities are what allowed for misinformation and silence to win out, then we have to break it. The reason I wrote that poem was because I was embarrassed to bits. But what is so embarrassing about being an ordinary girl? Why is it so shameful when someone else does something mean to you? It's all based on how we construct girlhood and womanhood. Anything that silence has allowed to grow and fester, we have to then vocalize. This thing happened with Hillary, and all these women began writing about their abuse, and how many times they've been groped, yelled at—this is all coming out on a national stage. Hillary said at one of the debates something like, "There's not a woman alive who doesn't know what this feels like," and everybody was like, "Right." And now the men in our lives—even the good men who are feminists—are absolutely astonished that this has been our reality. Now everyone's realizing that we're calling out rape culture. I didn't do it enough for your generation, and I am sorry.

How do we stop this? We keep talking about it and don't let ourselves be silenced or embarrassed. In practical terms, in life, when we see a friend or a woman who is too drunk at a bar and there's that guy who keeps getting her more drinks and she's falling down—you go stand next to him, you interrupt that. That's what you do. You interrupt it, call it out, take a picture of him, and say, "I don't know who this girl is, but I have this on my phone." Those are acts of tremendous bravery.

Some other ways? My five-year-old daughter takes karate twice a week. That may be cynical, or it may be empowering. I'm not sure which it is. I don't trust this world to change, and I want her to have some kind of power that she knows she has inside her body. I want her not only to be a kick-ass girl but to actually kick ass if she needs to.

NLT It's interesting in the poem "Postfeminism," the idea of how feminism has changed from your mother's generation to yours, and how in today's world the predator isn't always the masked man hiding in the bushes, but rather the classmate who drove you home from a party. We've been seeing those sorts of stories come out more and more.

BS It's the taboo and social cost for women for telling. Let's say a woman from the 1950s is getting walked home from a party, she's had three drinks, and she then is raped in her apartment. There was absolutely no recourse. If she was drunk and let him walk her home—she got what she deserved. If she got pregnant, guess what? She loses her job, she's kicked out of her apartment, and she has to go live in some strange unwed mothers' home, give birth to the baby, never see the baby again, and go back and try to make her life again. Absolutely no agency! And these weren't rapes from the bushes. These were colleagues, cousins, professors—and we have such a long way to go. Most women won't report a rape. The process they have to report is completely dehumanizing and humiliating all over again. They have to get every part of their body reexamined. They'll lose the rape kit. There's zero respect for the entire process. It's so much easier for a woman to be like, "Forget it, I'll take a shower and just forget this whole night."

I was talking to another poetry teacher, and she asked me, "What percentage of your female students do you think write about, talk about, or are dealing with sexual trauma?" I said, "Probably seven out of ten." And then two of our women students were next to us and each told us their stories, so nine out of ten? It's a constant battle, and as I said earlier it isn't just rape—it's the constant threat of rape. It's the constant fear that you're not supposed to do anything that someone can misinterpret as some reasonable way to get at you. And that means not wanting to go to the gym at night because you have to park in the parking garage. For millions of women all across the country, we have to mold our routine and thoughts around this threat. I mean, you're not able to go jogging. Jogging has become this flashpoint, like if you go jogging—just forget it. Whatever happens to you is your fault, because you had the nerve to go exercise at night. Oh, you got me started.

NLT Going in a different direction, something I've admired about your writing is the use of different tones. Sometimes you merge the lyrical and dense musicality with a detached matter-of-factness and colloquial aphorisms, which speaks to the double life of the poet and creates layers of emotions. "Last Sleep, Best Sleep" reads, "The great fruits of my failure: / silk milk pills with little bitter pits. / Who talks like that? Says we are / ever-locked, leaving everything petaled and veined the way nature / pretended." In these lines we get a clear break in the poetic voice and also a pun, which makes this somber poem humorous. This fusion happens line to line, poem to poem. How do you maintain a harmony between these voices? Is this something you think about, especially when writing long poems?

BS It comes from trying to create a variety of cultural sentence types. I think it's my job as a poet to find many different ways to be human. Sometimes we speak in a down-to-earth way because we need clarity and want to connect. Other times the thought is complicated, and we have to use slightly elevated or strange words. Mostly I believe in the idea that a poem is as complicated as it needs to be. When we are dealing with things that are so complex and possibly contradictory, and kind of a big mess of things—it's just not possible to write about them adequately in merely one register. It might need a vernacular tone, a more academic viewpoint, political feminist language, or a pop culture reference at that moment. I think our world has so many different voices competing all the time, and I don't see any reason not to use that to get at any truths they all may lead to.

NLT There's an interesting idea in *So Much Synth* of a generational hurt. I'm thinking of "I Have a Time Machine" in the lines, "Me exploding at my mother who explodes at me / because of the explosion / of some dark star all the way back struck hard / at mother's mother's mother." This is also apparent in "Dress Form": "Anyone / who hurts another was hurt that same way, / so how far back behind our backs do we go / to finally find the first hurt; whose finger / points to say, 'You! You're the one who god / knows why started a cycle of unending pain.'" Can you elaborate more of the cyclical wound between mother and daughter both not fitting the expectations of the other?

BS We think we know each other so well. We think we know, "I know how she is. I know if I do that, then she's going to do this." And it's very hard for one person to break it alone. But if you both figure out a way to say, "Let's not presume based on the past that I know what you're gonna do every single time in the future," if there's a way that one of you can break that expectation—let's say Mom baits you like she always does, and you take the bait. What happens next time if you don't take the bait and do something different? See if changing one part of the script can change the rest of it. The way hurts happen from mother to daughter is that mother is passing on hurts inflicted on her that were not examined.

Alice Miller's *The Drama of the Gifted Child* is about narcissistic parenting, meaning your parent can be either really evil and abusive, or they can be completely loving and do it for your own good. But the essence is when a parent needs the child to act a certain way and that becomes the most important thing, and the kid has no choice but to choose the love of the parent over what she needs to do. So, as a result, she chooses the approval of her parent because she cannot afford not to have that over anything else she wants to do. In this way the parent breaks the child, because the child has to suppress who she really is, and she becomes an adult who goes, "I have no idea what I want, why I want it." Her true self, and that's the gift—the gifted child isn't the intelligent child; the gifted child is the one who knows who she is. Now, you see how this connects with rape culture, right? These kinds of enforced rules and conformity are things she learned from her mom, so she thinks it's right. The way people think spanking is right—"Well, I was spanked!" And you never process that, so you don't realize how much damage it's done, and then you spank your kid, and they grow up and spank theirs. The only way you cannot pay it forward the exact same way—the spanking and narcissistic parenting—is to turn around and ask how your parents were parented. But you'll see from Alice Miller, the world protects parents, and especially children protect parents.

NLT I was wondering if you could speak to the balance of writing confessional and persona poems—using artifice as a liberating experience while creating a device, perhaps, to disguise or remove yourself, the poet, from the experience of the speaker. Are cheaters and liars the only ones who have a double life, or does the poet too?

BS Fiction writers have this hard line between fact and fiction, so they're understood to be like, "This is not me! This is a fictional tale!" Memoirists have the exact opposite and be like, "I have to prove that everything is true." Poets get to be somewhere in between. The only thing really protecting us, from both ourselves and our readers' expectations, is that little gap between the author and the speaker. The speaker of the poem cannot be collapsed into the author. So we can say the wildest things. And maybe someone says, "Did you really kill a man, boil his head, and serve it for dinner?" But this is a metaphor, so we get the satisfaction of having done this in text. And it's not a metaphor for peace and love, but one for violence and a revenge fantasy. It's a win-win. We can say whatever we want, and we can be protected in our truths, too. We can mix it all together so nobody knows what's what. The "I" works as a sort of pseudonym to keep that distance. The speaker in the poem "Our Andromeda" is a sort of shattered speaker, and she is very, very angry. I don't have to take the blame for being that angry person. I have protection if someone wants to call me out and be like, "It's so rude for you to be angry at the wrong people." And it's like, that's that speaker. She has every right to feel how that speaker feels. It's a tremendous tool.

NLT The poem "Visitor" reminds me very much of Dickinson's "I dwell in Possibility," in the way that it uses the imagination to transform the domestic sphere and merges it with natural imagery, creating a house of poetry that has trees, sun, and "leaf light." The final lines, "Like a dark book in a long life with a vague / hope in a wood house with an open door," have this almost anxious rhythm and conclude with an iambic release through "an open door." I think this use of meter to create a resonating harmony or disjunction is something that Dickinson's rhythm often does. Another similarity is the image of the door, as this metaphysical portal into the imagination. Can you speak a bit about influences—ways in which you channel another poet or pickpocket something you admire?

BS I don't do that consciously. I've internalized Dickinson's exhortation, like when I say myself, I do not mean me, I mean a supposed person—that is what I believe in. I've also internalized Whitman's "I contain multitudes," like I believe in all of that. How do I use my reading, and how does it get into my work? I don't really know. That process is mysterious. Somebody—I'm not sure who—said if a line comes to you whole, you might want to research it because it might be somebody else's line.

That poem in particular was guided by longing. It was just yearning for the company of a particular friend. The inspiration was what I could come up with as a bridge, or a lure, for this friend to come. Part of that bridge was a particularly seductive way of using prepositional phrases. When you're speaking to other writers, there's a way that we know what they like, because we know what they write. I don't know. This is a funny question because, for me, I didn't steal any patterns from Dickinson for that poem. It's lovely that you read that influence, because it's one that's there, but I didn't do it consciously.

NLT Who are some artists you think have duende?

BS Some poets who have serious, serious duende are Robin Coste Lewis, Rachel McKibbens, Natalie Diaz, and Jericho Brown. As far as visual artists go, one of the most beautiful things I've seen in a long time is that film *Moonlight.* It is a game changer. I also think the Iranian-American painter, mixed-media artist Toba Khedoori is a really interesting person. Those are some people I'm thinking about lately. Oh! Hilton Als is one of the best, best, best writers on the planet. You read his pieces in the *New Yorker*, his reviews on film and theater, and you're like, "Who wrote this masterpiece?! Oh, Hilton. Of course." Every turn of phrase is stunning.

NLT Sweet. I'll have to check him out. I'd like to end on a simple question. What is your "internal landscape"?

BS That is the most complex question. My internal landscape is probably a mixture of dreams and past landscapes. Not the actual landscapes of my childhood, but the way my childhood landscapes come up in dreams. Probably things like my high school hallways, and my kids' school hallways, and just the way you wear a path. For example, I lived in an apartment with my family in New York City for five years, and it was like there were these worn grooves in the sidewalk I would see when I'd go the same way every single day. I have a sense that some deep part of my brain is lined with those brownstones. And now we live in a house in New Jersey, and I feel like my landscape is an innerscape, although there is more sky. I'm thinking of one of those View-Masters with all the little discs—that at any given moment or time might change. But generally my landscape, when I'm alone in my thoughts, and I'm not reading anything, so I'm not getting any input and not trying to process anything, just in my head is a truly private blend of wishing to be nothingness. You know, if you try to think of nothing in some kind of Zen meditation it's impossible—it's just pop-up after pop-up. Who comes up often? It's not a scene. It's a who in my landscape—the faces of my kids, the sudden realization I've said something stupid, or terrible, or wrong, and I'll look at that person's face in my mind for a while, wondering if I should make a call. There is some landscape—sort of sky, sort of street, sort of faces—nothing all that calm.

A Conversation with Elizabeth Strout

SAMANTHA VORWALD

Elizabeth Strout is no stranger to literary honors. Her first novel, Amy and Isabelle, *was shortlisted for the 2000 Orange Prize and was a finalist for the PEN/Faulkner Award. In 2009, her collection of connected stories,* Olive Kitteridge, *won the Pulitzer Prize for fiction. Her sixth novel,* Anything is Possible, *was published this year to much acclaim. She recently visited Butler University as part of the Vivian S. Delbrook Visiting Writers Series and read from her 2016 bestseller,* My Name Is Lucy Barton. *The next day, she sat down with* Booth *to talk about crafting characters, facing rejection, and drawing material from daily life.*

Samantha Vorwald In *Olive Kitteridge* and your novel *My Name Is Lucy Barton,* your characters seem so real, and the pieces almost read as non-fiction. I had to remind myself that they are indeed fiction. Is there any relationship between the characters and people in your real life?

Elizabeth Strout Not really. There's a part of me in every character I write, whether it's male or female, because everything has to go through me. Everything I've observed or heard or whatever—it all has to go through me. I'm the one who makes these people up, and so there's a part of me in some form in all of these people, but I really have made them up. But they're so real to me, you know? By the time I'm done with them on the page, they're very, very real to me. They're just as real to me as anybody that I've ever met. So that's hopefully what you're feeling.

SV In *My Name Is Lucy Barton,* she says that she can't write about her own marriage, and she says that it isn't a book about her marriage or why it failed. But she seems so honest and upfront about other sensitive topics. Is this because you didn't want the book to become about marriage, or is it because you feel that more closely matches Lucy's character, to not want to write about her own marriage?

ES Well, both. It's all one and the same, actually, because this is about Lucy and about her crossing class lines. It's about what that feels like, and it's a lot about what her childhood did to her. So as I started to put it all together, I realized if the marriage is going to be there, it will take over in a certain way. And I just didn't want that to happen. I thought, "Okay, then let's just have Lucy state it straight out to the reader." Her voice is honest, and there's a purity, I think, to the voice. And so I thought, "Let's just say straight to the reader this isn't going to be the story of my marriage," and so that kind of solved it for me. And then I could stick in the few details that I wanted to about the marriage, but I realized that would be a different story or would make her story lopsided in a way. Marriage is a huge deal. And, you know, she'd been married for a while, and I just thought, "All right, then let's just not do that. Let's just say we're not going to talk about it," which is Lucy's voice.

SV Lucy's friend Jeremy tells her to be "ruthless" as a writer. Have you at times been ruthless as a writer, and would you advise this for other writers, as well?

ES You know, it's interesting, that word. I had Jeremy use it, and it sounded right to me. It sounded like something that Jeremy, with his different funny little complexities, would say. But it's not a word I would use. And yet now that I've written it, I think that one does have to be ruthless, I guess. I guess what I would say is, if you're going to be a writer, if you really want to be a writer, then you need to arrange your life around that. And that may appear ruthless to other people or it may not. I think, especially if you're a man, it doesn't really appear ruthless. You're just doing your thing. This isn't really about gender except that I said that, but I think that if you really want to do this, then you've got to do what it takes to do it.

SV How do you think that might appear for other writers, or is it different for everybody?

ES Well, I think it's got to be different for everybody because there are particular circumstances. And now I'm going to go back to the gender thing, actually, because I think it's more difficult for women to say, "All right, this is what I'm going to do. This is what I need. I need six hours a day by myself, and I might need twenty years of nothing ever getting published." And who's going to want to put up with that? But if you need to do that, you need to do that. Whereas I think it's easier for a man to say, "This is what I'm going to do. Bye."

SV Why do you say it's easier for a man to do it?

ES I think that historically it's been easier for a man to go into another room and close the door and say, "Okay, I'm not coming out for six hours." I think it's just easier for the man to have done that, in the past. It's changing, obviously, thank goodness. But yes, I think everybody has to find their own form of ruthlessness. But you've got to do it. That's my point. If you want to do it, you've got to do it.

SV Your books and stories are not exactly dramatic in the sense of explosions and everything, but there is a powerful synergy that compels the reader forward. Can you articulate how this synergy would develop in a story?

ES I really believe in the sentence. Every sentence has to have some heartbeat of life to it. Every sentence that gets put down has to come from the sentence before it and lead into the sentence that's coming after. There has to be a "wholeness" at work, and there has to be a heartbeat in every sentence, if that makes sense. And it's not easy to learn to do. I trained myself over the years to get rid of any sentence that's dead weight. And so I think maybe that's what you're talking about, hopefully. That would be the business that carries it forward.

SV The driving force.

ES Yeah, because when I write, it's very aural. My ear is very, very important to me. So the sentence has to land on the ear the right way, and then if that is landing on the reader's ear the right way, they will be carried forward. But it's something I've learned to hear and learned to do and to get rid of every twig—what I call twigs—every dead piece of wood. Just get it out of there.

SV I was at your reading last night. When you're reading out loud in front of everybody, does it still hit you the same way on your own ears as it did when you were writing it?

ES If I'm lucky. If I'm lucky, yes. I don't read out loud that often. You know, I will read it to myself out loud at times. I used to read out loud to myself a lot, but then I began to understand that I could cheat myself and make it sound like it was good and it wasn't. So I've cut back on reading aloud. Now I'm making sure my ears are actually hearing it in my head.

SV Did you ever consider being something other than a writer? I know you were an attorney for six months.

ES Yes, horrible, horrible. Awful . . . You know, I really never did. I had an awful long period of time before my work was accepted into the world. And there was one period of time back then when I'd probably been writing for about fifteen years with very little—a few stories here and there—but very little acknowledgment. And I did think to myself, "I have to stop. It's just not making sense." So I decided to go to nursing school. I was teaching at Manhattan Community College at the time, and there was a nursing program, so I went down to the nursing program and said I would like to apply. And they said, "Okay, well, here's the application." And the application was so confusing that I just thought, "Oh, forget it. I'm just going to stick to being a writer." That's the truth. I just couldn't even figure out the application, and I just didn't even really want to do it. But I just felt, "This isn't working," and then by the end of that day I thought, "No, too bad, I'm just going to try this story one more time—try it a different way." And then there was one other time when I thought I would have to give it up, but I didn't think "Oh, I'll be a nurse" or anything. It lasted about twenty-four hours, and then I thought, "Well, let me try this story this way." So I'm always, always going back and trying it one more time. But it was a long, discouraging time.

SV What is it that you enjoy about writing fiction?

ES You know, here's my favorite thing about writing fiction. When I write—when I go to the page—I suspend judgment on my characters. And in real life, I'm sure I'm probably as judgmental as most people in real life. I try not to be, but, you know, it's how we manage to make our way through life. We just make our judgments. But when I go to the page, I am so free of judgment of my characters, and that's so fun. It's so liberating because I don't care how badly behaved they are—as long as they're truthfully bad behaved, I don't care. So I just love them, and they can do whatever they need to do, and I'm free from judgment. That's my favorite part.

SV What writers do you find yourself returning to for either joy or inspiration?

ES Always the Russians. I've always loved the Russians. I love Tolstoy. I love him. And I love his short stories. I love *War and Peace,* I love *Anna Karenina,* and I love Tolstoy. And so I do go back to him every so often. And Chekhov, I love Chekhov. I mean, I just love the Russians, so they're always there for me. And I love John Cheever, I love Updike, I love Philip Roth, I love Alice Munro, William Trevor. Those are sort of my standbys. Virginia Woolf.

SV In your writing process, what do you struggle with the most, and how do you get past or work around that?

ES What I struggle with the most—it tends to happen about halfway through making a book, because I don't write from beginning to end. I don't worry about plot because I'm just always writing these different scenes, and they'll eventually connect in some way. However, before they're actually connecting or before that has solidified enough, there's a stretch of time where I feel like a washing machine where all the soap is coming out the doors. I feel like, "Oh, oh, oh dear, oh dear." I just feel like I'm out of control of it, that I'll never be able to pull it together in a structure that's needed. And that can last for months, and that's a difficult period because it makes me feel crazy with anxiety. I want to get it into a place where I can work, and so there's always that period sort of midway through. Then I do eventually get it sorted out, even though every single time it feels like I won't. It's interesting. Every time, at that particular phase of it, I think, "Ugh, this isn't going to happen." But then it does. But that's the most uncomfortable part.

SV As you mentioned earlier, you took a lot of rejection at the beginning of your writing career. I'm wondering what was going through your head. What would you say to writers who are facing the same rejection struggles?

ES Well, I'm the poster child for rejections. I was forty-three when my first book was published. I remember hearing Raymond Carver say that he kept writing long past the time when it made sense to stop. And I did the math, and I realized, "Okay, I've gone a lot longer than you." So I really did go a long time without much acknowledgment. But what kept me going was that I just wanted to do it. And also what kept me going was I understood intuitively that my work wasn't yet good enough. I always understood that. So there were people who were saying, "Well, you should go have lunch with that guy at the *New Yorker* that's nice to you." And I was like, "Why would I want to have lunch with him? My work isn't good enough." What's the point of talking somebody into publishing a story? I didn't want that. I wanted my work to be good! And I understood that it wasn't quite good enough, but I also understood that it was getting better. So that was helpful to me. And then there was an editor at the *New Yorker* for fifteen years who kept rejecting my stories, but his rejection letters kept getting longer and longer, and he was helpful to me. But mostly I was just always trying. I just kept trying. I understood it wasn't good enough, I understood that it was within reach, and I just had to keep going. And I was surprised that it was taking me so long. I just thought, "Ugh, boy, I had no idea you'd be this slow." But I did eventually figure out how to get those sentences down in the right way. I figured out how to make a muscular sentence that could carry all the stuff it needed to carry.

SV So you think it's down to just the power of the sentence alone?

ES I do. I mean, not that anything is separate, because it's always the whole, but you can't have a piece of writing, I think—and people disagree with this—but I do not think you can have a piece of writing that's worth anything without every sentence being good. Every sentence.

SV Last night at your reading, you said that writers should write about the things that aren't normally written about or spoken about. And later you explained that some of the names came directly from your own family members, that you would combine them with a separate family name, like your Aunt Olive and then the Kitteridge family name. I was wondering, what would you say to writers who have a difficult character they want to write, but it's based on somebody they know?

ES You know, I think go ahead and do it. Just go ahead and do it. Because, first of all, when you think you're writing about somebody, the moment you begin to write, it's not that person. You may think that you're using this person, but on the page they become different automatically. It's so interesting. So you're not actually writing about that person, but if that person has something to say in your life that's helpful for you, do it. Write it.

I think it's a very, very good question, because I think it's what keeps young writers from daring to write. They feel like they could lose the relationship if they wrote honestly. Joan Didion said writers are always selling somebody out. I'm not sure I would put it that way, but I really think that, as I said before, if you're using somebody, they're going to be different immediately on the page even if they feel that they've been used. They're not. They're just different.

But the other thing—the most important thing I think a young writer needs to know—is that it's yourself you're going to be revealing. So you may worry that you're going to base it on somebody else, but it's always yourself that you're really revealing, and that's very hard to take. You know, I remember somebody saying, "Being a writer is like standing in the middle of the turnpike without your underpants on." Oh, god! And I always remembered that because there's some truth to it. But you know what? If you can get over that, then you can write anything. Like my mother once said, "So how can you write about life if you're not going to write about life?" And it was so great because, yeah, use everything that comes your way. Just use it. And understand that people may not like it, and that's okay. But you've got to do it. And the person will change anyway. But that's what I would say. Go for it, go for it, go for it. Now that sounds ruthless.

A Conversation with Meghan Daum

SUSAN LERNER

Meghan Daum's opinion column in the Los Angeles Times *has run for more than a decade, but my first encounter with her work was "My Misspent Youth," a piece the* New Yorker *ran in 1999 that became the titular essay for her first collection. Daum also penned the memoir* Life Would Be Perfect If I Lived in That House *and a novel,* The Quality of Life Report. *The anthology she edited,* Selfish, Shallow, and Self-Absorbed: Sixteen Writers on the Decision Not to Have Kids, *became a* New York Times *bestseller. Her most recent collection of essays,* The Unspeakable: And Other Subjects of Discussion, *won the 2015 PEN Center USA Award for creative nonfiction.*

In 2015 Daum received a Guggenheim Fellowship, and in 2016 she received a National Endowment for the Arts Fellowship. She is an adjunct associate professor in the MFA Writing Program at Columbia University's School of the Arts and is currently the Bedell Distinguished Visiting Professor in the University of Iowa's Nonfiction Writing Program. Her work has appeared in some of the country's most esteemed publications, and last year she began a column called "Egos" for the Sunday New York Times Book Review.

Daum's essays center on the theme of what constitutes authentic living. The pieces in The Unspeakable *explore the tension that arises when society's ex-*

pectations of how we should live and feel differ from our true experiences and feelings.

Daum, a recent writer-in-residence in the Butler University MFA program, sat down with Booth *to discuss identity politics, cultural appropriation, and the wisdom of wearing tiny sombreros to tequila parties.*

Susan Lerner In "The Joni Mitchell Problem," one of the essays from *The Unspeakable,* you contrasted "letting it all hang out" with "putting yourself out there." You wrote that "putting yourself out there" doesn't foist a confession on the audience as much as let it in on a secret that is turned into a story. A lot of people are writing confessional essays from the "the personal is the political" stance. Can you speak to this?

Meghan Daum Sometimes the personal isn't the political. Sometimes the personal is just personal. I really like the idea of making a distinction between confessing and confiding. I can't take credit for this—Emily Fox Gordon, a wonderful essayist, talks about this. I've borrowed this idea from her. Confessing puts the onus on the reader. I think when you write something unbaked, kind of spewing, that's releasing a torrent of ideas, revealing stuff about yourself in an unthoughtful, unchecked way, even if there's something sort of prurient and entertaining about it, it's not really good writing and it's not a good literary experience. Because what you're asking the reader to do is forgive you. To confess is to ask for forgiveness. That's not the job of the reader. I really think you get your confessing out of the way in the first couple of drafts, and then hopefully by the time you have something that's finished or publishable it's going to be an intimacy that's conveyed through confiding. You want your reader to feel you're offering her something. You don't want the reader to feel a great burden is placed upon her.

SL How do you get from confessing to confiding?

MD You present the reader with something you've thought all the way through. Like: I had this experience. I'm going to tell you the details in a way that's personal, but I'm going to present this to you as a set of ideas and in a narrative that I'm controlling. You want to give them a finished product rather than a stream of consciousness. It's really the difference between having something that's raw and that's cooked.

SL Lionel Shriver contributed to your anthology, *Selfish, Shallow, and Self-Absorbed*. Earlier this year at the Brisbane Writers Festival in Australia, she argued against the concept of cultural appropriation while wearing a sombrero, which was said to be a nod to an incident at Bowdoin College at which non-Mexican students were disciplined for wearing tiny sombreros at a tequila party. In the *Guardian*, Yassmin Abdel-Magied slammed Shriver for normalizing the ideas behind colonialism. In the *New Republic*, Phoebe Maltz Bovy wrote a nuanced piece that conceded that Shriver had valid points. What are your thoughts on cultural appropriation?

MD Well, I do think that Lionel Shriver has some valid points. We're in a really intense moment right now where cultural and racial and identity tensions are running very high in lots of different ways on campuses and elsewhere. I think that in some cases—and not all—there has been an over-correction. I do think this notion that a fiction writer, especially, cannot write in the persona of a character that is not exactly the same as she is, is absurd, and I think that's what Lionel was getting at. The substance of her talk I agree with. I think it's pretty unassailable. The fact that she's wearing a sombrero, that's Lionel. She's a provocateur. It would not have been something I would have done, and I do think the sombrero and some of the rhetoric she employed eclipsed the core meaning of the speech. It's no secret that I am very much of the belief that identity politics—and people tend to have different ideas about what that term actually means—has limited uses. It does have some uses, absolutely, good uses. But they're not as extensive as some people think. Human beings are complex, which means speech can be complex and therefore easily messed up and misconstrued. But free speech is paramount.

SL It is complex. You're talking about identity politics, and there was this piece in the *New York Times* by . . .

MD Mark Lilla.

SL Yeah. I see his points. But it seems to me that marginalized people have never felt heard, so how do we remedy that if we put identity politics at a lower tier?

MD I think there's a difference between not wanting this thing we're calling identity politics to be the engine of every discussion and just saying something glib like "Down with identity politics!" People have the identities that they have. And people express what they express and write what they write. But the danger of identity politics is when people use them to make rules about who's allowed to talk about what, when people start saying, "You are different from me, and therefore you cannot understand anything about me, you don't know where I'm coming from, and we cannot co-exist in the same space." Now, many people I know and respect deeply would tell me I'm off base on this. But part of the problem is that nobody can really agree on what identity politics means and how it manifests. We're having a situation in classrooms right now where language is sometimes over-policed, and students are leading with a level of sensitivity that is very well intended but often not helpful. At its worst, it can completely overwhelm any sort of intellectual discourse. It can allow emotions to overwhelm people's ability to think critically and independently. Because, look, it's possible to do two things at once. It's possible to be sensitive to people's experiences, to acknowledge histories of oppression and systems of oppression, and also to say, "Hey, we're all here. Let's have a free conversation and not have to be constantly checking ourselves and looking over our shoulders as to what we're saying." Otherwise, you can't get anywhere.

SL I'm going to riff on the whole unfortunate sombrero wardrobe choice, which made me think of the Halloween controversy at Yale. Its Intercultural Affairs Committee sent out a note asking that students be thoughtful about culturally themed costumes. When the associate head of Yale's Silliman College criticized this letter, minority students criticized her, and she ended up resigning her post as lecturer. What are your thoughts on this?

MD I'm not a person of color, so I would not presume . . . I understand that people feel a certain way about that. All I can say . . . The fact that I'm parsing my words so carefully is just so indicative of the delicacy here. I guess I would say that it doesn't speak well for our society that students from marginalized groups can feel so undermined and unseen and disrespected in general that something like a Halloween costume—a costume that is maybe tone deaf but not malicious in intent—can be so harmful. I'm not denying their experience. I'm just sorry we're living in that kind of world.

SL I'm playing devil's advocate here. If you were Native American and someone showed up in the cliché feather-on-the-headband costume, that might be . . . Or, for instance, I'm Jewish. If someone showed up dressed as an old shtetl rabbi, I don't know how I'd feel about that.

MD I guess maybe the question is, is there a difference between students having a conversation among themselves about how they feel about something like Halloween costumes, and having the university instituting a policy that you cannot wear these costumes? It goes back to this whole in loco parentis question: How much authority should a university exert, and to what degree should students use the college experience as a way of figuring out what bothers them and what doesn't, and how to talk about it with other people, and how to navigate it?

SL Maybe if we were people of color on a college campus we would dread Halloween. Or if we were Native American and saw all these Native American costumes, we would not feel as though we had a voice until the university assisted by saying, "Hey, let's look at this and be respectful of one another."

MD That could be. In that case, I would love to read something by a Native American talking about how he or she dreads Halloween every year. Maybe this is a common experience. I haven't read it. I would like to read that piece and hear that perspective. Didn't they conduct surveys that found that most Native Americans are fine with keeping the Washington Redskins' nickname?

SL My sense is that very few people are aware these polls were flawed, and I think it's important more people know this.

MD Really? Interesting. I'll read up on that.

SL I'm going to move on to something else. You reviewed Didion's *Blue Nights* for the *Los Angeles Review of Books*. You wrote that the book was less a story than a series of effects, and you wondered why Didion wasn't being called out for her "relentless opacity." As someone who writes in the tradition of Didion, can you talk about what it was like to write and publish that review?

MD It was good. That was a really interesting project that the *L.A. Review of Books* did because they had five different people review that book. They ran the reviews on consecutive days. I think I was fourth out of five. I wasn't the only one to say, "I can't believe she even wrote it." It was an incredibly difficult thing for her to do. I think she basically says in the book, about three-quarters of the way through, "I'm done with it. I'm stopping. I can't write this anymore." She kind of gives up, and that's kind of the effect of the book. She sort of turns that surrender into a literary gesture. I liked writing that piece. It wasn't just about the book but about her whole body of work. The degree to which my work has been compared to hers— that is something that happens to any woman writer of a certain kind of nonfiction. The comparison I made is that women singer-songwriters are compared to Joni Mitchell just because her sound is so infectious, and as musicians are developing their craft it gets into their ears. It's also true of Didion. She was so revelatory, the way she put sentences together—often opaque, but in her early work not as much—and the sort of sound that she had. A lot of us internalized it as we were growing up and reading and figuring out how to write. She's at the end of her career now. I applaud her for even getting that book out into the world. There was a biography of her I reviewed for the *Atlantic*, and I wrote a lot about her work in that, too. And I've interviewed her. I've met her.

SL In a podcast hosted by Anna David called *You've Got Issues*, you re-marked negatively about women's groups that are architected to help women overcome implicit sexism in the workplace. Women writers on Facebook have formed groups called binders for this purpose. I've noticed that you are in one of the binders.

MD I probably am.

SL I assume you're not very active, but I want to ask you what your take is on the binders.

MD It's hard to say because it got so big! First it was a tiny binder and then it exploded.

SL And now there's a million sub-binders.

MD Yeah, a million. I think I have kind of a strange experience as a woman. I'm interested in the idea of psychological androgyny. For what-ever reason, I am not somebody who generally sees the world or my life primarily through the lens of my gender. I understand that I might be an outlier in that way, and I understand that's maybe not a typical experience, but I don't feel a great connection to that sort of group. But then again I don't like any groups. I never want to be in any club. I'm sort of allergic to groups. And trends. I don't like groups or trends. The direction that feminism sometimes can go in this moment in time I find frustrating. I say that as a feminist.

SL What is . . .

MD There is this kind of generic "You go, girl," "I'm a badass" attitude, and all it takes to be a badass apparently is getting up every morning and getting dressed and facing down the patriarchy. It just seems a little bit too easy. It kind of goes back to this identity politics thing. I would like to see a world in which people interact more on the substance and less on the baggage they have decided to acquire. That is an oversimplified way of summing up a multi-dimensional phenomenon, but I'll leave it there for now.

SL Is it clinging to a sense of victimhood, you're getting at?

MD There is that element. And the thing is, obviously people deal with trauma in their own ways. I would never say that you should downplay or deny or not deal with things that have happened to you. Never. But sometimes there is a sense of leading with the trauma, and that approach doesn't resonate with me, personally. And I am interested in the way that feminism has been, I think, sort of watered down by this obsession with how difficult it is to be a woman and how undermined we are at every turn. And how men are either mansplaining or manspreading or being terrible oppressors left and right. I don't think that's happening all the time. I just don't. I think it's sometimes happening, but there are many more moving pieces than that. Life is more complicated than that.

SL I feel like there's a great comeback question here, and it's not coming to me.

MD There would be many, many people who would argue with me when I talk about this kind of thing. But I also think there would be many people who agree with me. It's hard to talk about this stuff right now.

SL True. Okay, let's go back. What are your thoughts about Yale students' requests that campus buildings named for slave owners be renamed?

MD I am not an administrator at Yale. I do not have a position on that.

SL Okay. I just keep picturing a student of color walking into one of those buildings named for an owner of slaves.

MD Right. The question is, how far does this go?

SL So do you do nothing . . .

MD Or do you do a little bit, or do you do everything? I'm not the one to answer these questions.

SL Okay, one more question about this. In your column about racial unrest at Yale and Mizzou, you wrote, "Can we find a way to make intellectual spaces and safe spaces one and the same?" At the height of the conflict at Mizzou, students created a safe space and, along with a teacher, physically barred a journalist from entering the area. What are your feelings about this?

MD Well, that's not fair. You can't do that. Why are they afraid to have the journalist? They should want the journalist to go in and talk to them and find out what's going on.

SL Well, one would think that. I have read that minority students have historically felt betrayed by the media. Not given a fair shake in having their voices heard, and that their stories have been slanted. So what they wanted was to not have to deal with journalists in their safe space at the height of the tension.

MD Sorry, no, I don't buy that. I found it ironic that the teacher who helped block the journalist was a communications professor or media professor or something like that. If you have an issue and you're having a protest, you can't just selectively choose what media's going to come in. That's what Donald Trump is doing right now. This is the same playbook. No. This is freedom of the press. This is freedom of speech. If you can't handle having your story reported then you can't complain about anything. I will not give any slack on that one.

SL In a *Live Talks Los Angeles* podcast you made in 2014, you interviewed Francine Prose and asked her if she believed writing can be taught. As a student in the MFA program here at Butler, I was kind of crushed to hear her emphatically say no, as I was when I read Jo Ann Beard and Vivian Gornick say the same thing. As someone who has an MFA and teaches in an MFA program, how do you see your role as teacher and how would you answer the same question?

MD I'm not an academic. That's not my world. I come from the journalism world. My approach when I teach is, I say, "I'm your editor. You guys are the writers. You're going to treat me like your editor and vice versa, and I'm going to help you figure out what kind of writer you are, what kind of stuff you're interested in, how you want to shape whatever is in front of you so you can reach the kind of audience you want. We'll work as a team." That's what I can bring to the table. Whether or not that counts as teaching them to write? I think it's teaching them how to make the most out of the material that they have and the sensibility that they have, and then figure out how they want to do it. To that extent I would say it can be taught. Can you actually be taught to have talent? Obviously not. That's in any discipline. Can math be taught? Not to me!

SL So you're saying the craft elements . . .

MD Yeah, the craft elements, and training your brain to see the world in such a way that you're thinking about how you're going to respond to it. That's because that's my particular background and my particular sensibility. Somebody else would have a different approach. Francine Prose and Vivian Gornick and Jo Ann Beard . . . why would they say that?

SL It's really crushing. [Laughs.]

SL Okay. So, in "Haterade," a piece you wrote for the *Believer* in 2012, you wrote that the Internet has facilitated a degeneration of the state of social discourse. Here we are, less than a month after the election. Facebook friends who voted differently are unfriending each other. Many in the "I'm With Her" camp say that anyone who voted for Trump is by definition a racist. In February, in your column about [Ruth Bader] Ginsburg and [Antonin] Scalia's friendship, you wrote, "Tolerance has become something of a lost art. Instead we dig in our heels and declare sides." What are your feelings about the way those of us not in favor of our current president-elect speak about those who voted for Trump?

MD It takes two to tango, right? We don't like it when they say all sorts of terrible things about [Barack] Obama and liberals, and I can't imagine they like it when we reduce every discussion to calling them racist or misogynist. Ultimately, I think that racism and sexism and various other -isms and phobias played a role in the election, but at the end of the day it's just not that simple. There was a huge constellation of factors in play. Historians will spend the next hundred years trying to figure it out.

SL It's a complicated thing.

MD It's interesting because Obama ran a campaign that was about transcending race. And he got a lot of people to vote for him based on that. He was the anti-identity-politics candidate. And that whole movement was so exciting to people, I think, because the idea was that we were "post-racial" now. But that was naïve, of course, and under his administration racial tensions escalated. I think he has handled himself so magnificently, throughout not only his administration but also the last three weeks. I know people on the other side who seem to think he somehow engendered these racial tensions. I don't really see how. But the fact is that Hillary ran a campaign that was using identity politics. She thought that leading with the pussy-grabbing meme was the way to go, and, frankly, so did everybody else, including me. When I watched that second debate and Trump was following her around and hovering over her, my reaction was, "Yes, we got him! This will not be tolerated! He's finished!" I know people who were very triggered by that and very upset, and I get it. But there was part of me that thought it would be amazing if he would try to physically attack her right on stage. Because the Secret Service was right there. She'd be totally safe. And it would be fantastic [because it would mean the end of his candidacy]. But we were just so wrong. They [Trump supporters] actually didn't care about that. He probably would have gotten even more votes if he'd physically attacked her. That's how clueless we were about the way he was being perceived. One of my best friends is a Christian conservative. She voted for Trump. We couldn't agree less on the issues, but we deeply love each other. A few days after the election, I talked to her on the phone for four hours. And she said, "You know, I listen to an audiotape like that, and it's so lame. I can't take this seriously. It's just so dumb."

SL The . . .

MD The *Access Hollywood* tape.

SL Oh. She didn't think that was a big deal?

MD No, she didn't.

SL And she can't be the only one who . . .

MD Were there people who didn't like Hillary because she's a woman? Yes. But they also don't like her because she's Hillary. People profoundly don't like the Clintons. I love them, personally, and I really like her. But I get it. This is an establishment candidate. I think that if there had been a woman out there telling those Trump voters what they wanted to hear, a lot of them would have voted for her. I wrote a column recently saying that the first black president could only have been like Obama. He's perfect. He's so many things at once. He's not even totally black. And the female analogue to that is the first woman president has to be not even totally a woman. You'd basically have to be a cyborg. There's no woman who can check all the required boxes and be all of the required things. Then a number of people wrote to me and said, "No, Condoleezza Rice could."

SL Oh, my god!

MD Yeah. I get that a lot from readers, actually. Conservative voters tell me they love Condoleezza Rice. But she's not married, and she doesn't have a family—I think that would knock her out of contention right away. But it's very interesting to me that a lot of Republicans think Rice is fantastic and are able to deal with a black woman, at least that particular black woman, no problem. So it's not just about race and gender. It's about personality, it's about appearance, it's about your platform—it's about so many things. And that takes us back to the ways that identity politics can be limiting. You're having a conversation and it's going, "As a person of color, I think this . . ." or "As a woman, I think this . . ." Enough already! You want to talk about intersectionality? Well, how about "We're all many things"? We're all oppressed in certain ways, and we're all privileged in certain ways. That's why I hope we can get to a moment where we're not obsessing over Halloween costumes because there are so many bigger fish to fry.

SL We've become so much more divided now.

MD Yeah! And this is not the time for it. Getting back to your question, what's upset me is not only the people who voted for Trump versus the other people, but within the liberals, now we're fighting each other. You're not outraged in the right way. You're not outraged enough. You're not accusing every Trump voter of being a racist; well then, you don't get it. You have internalized misogyny. Hey, don't tell me what I've internalized!

[Laughs.] Believe me, I can hate myself in all sorts of ways! It doesn't have to be gender specific!

SL So, I want to ask a follow-up about cultural appropriation. Some people think that white men, for instance, shouldn't write about, let's say, Nigerian women. That they shouldn't write across culture or race, because then the people they're writing about can't write their own stories. It's harder for them to get recognized, harder for them to get published, all these barriers they have to overcome. And meanwhile people who are more privileged, like us, who don't have to face those things, can more easily write those stories and profit from them.

MD In all likelihood a non-Nigerian person is not going to do as good, or at least the same, kind of job as a Nigerian person in writing the story of a Nigerian person. Still, everyone should write the story they want to write. Like I've said, I think the idea that you can only write your own story is incredibly limiting. We're talking about fiction, right? We're talking about novels. We're not talking about assuming a fake identity and writing a memoir.

SL I think that argument premises that the playing field is even.

MD I think it's more even than it's ever been. If you're talking about this particular moment, there's a huge appetite for all sorts of voices.

SL For global stories.

MD Yeah. If a Nigerian author writes an amazing book and for some reason the publisher buys a mediocre book by a white author writing about a Nigerian person, that's inexcusable. And I'd be surprised to see that happen at this particular moment, unless it was some incredibly famous, guaranteed bestselling white author. Now, has it happened in the past? Yes, but publishing is becoming more inclusive. Maybe not fast enough, but it's getting there. However, the idea of making rules for what an artist can do creatively is hugely worrisome. Everyone has his or her own unique story. To say that an artist who uses her imagination and writes beyond her own experience is committing "cultural appropriation" is to basically say that any given person's story is nothing more than some set of monolithic ideas about racial or gender or cultural identity. That's insulting.

SL There's an argument that maybe there's only so much room in the marketplace for this kind of story. So if I write a fiction story about a Nigerian woman, then the Nigerian woman's story might have less chance of being published.

MD You should ask a publisher, actually. An editor would be better to talk to about that.

SL My sense is that it's almost like affirmative action. That all this has happened in the past, so even though the playing field is more even than it has ever been, that we should make more room for these stories, because none of these stories have seen the light of day.

MD But I think that there's a difference between the publishing community being aware of the variety of stories out there and making an effort to include more people, and issuing some kind of decree that artists should only tell their own stories. That's just completely antithetical to art. That doesn't mean you're going to do a good job writing the story about the Nigerian person if you're a white American who's never been to Nigeria. But to make a rule that you can't do it? . . . It's kind of like the Halloween costume thing. Should you go as an American Indian for Halloween? That's between you and your moral compass. But, guess what? The ACLU says it's okay to go for Halloween as a Klansman! . . . You can't just legislate this stuff. If you start deciding en masse what's okay and what's not okay in terms of speech or creative expression, it takes the onus off individuals to have some kind of sense of compassion and some authority over their own moral system.

SL In an interview that just came out in *Slate*, Zadie Smith took issue with the concept of cultural appropriation. She said something like, "It offends me that people think I would be so vulnerable and crumble if somebody wrote my story."

MD I totally agree. We're all allowed to fail as artists. You can't deny a person the opportunity to do a really bad job at something. You can't deny them the opportunity to be offensive and mess up, to figure out what works and what doesn't work. Because that's the name of the game. Fail with all your heart.

CONTRIBUTORS

Kaitlyn Andrews-Rice received her MFA in creative writing from American University, where she served as editor-in-chief for *Folio*. She is the editor of *Split Lip Magazine* and her fiction is forthcoming in *Copper Nickel*. Find her roaming the beaches north of Boston with her husband, son, and pug, or online at thelegitkar.com or @thelegitkar.

Melissa Llanes Brownlee is a writer born and raised in Hawaii. She graduated from the University of Nevada, Las Vegas, with an MFA in fiction. She then moved to Japan to teach English, where she continues to do so. Her work has appeared in the *Waccamaw, The Jet Fuel Review, Crack the Spine, The Baltimore Review, River River,* and *The Notre Dame Review.*

Tara Campbell is a Washington, DC-based writer. In 2016 she was the grateful recipient of two awards from the DC Commission on the Arts and Humanities: the Larry Neal Writer's Award and the Mayor's Arts Award for Outstanding New Artist. She's an assistant fiction editor at *Barrelhouse*, volunteer with children's literacy organization 826DC, and MFA candidate at American University. Her debut novel, *TreeVolution*, was published in November 2016. Visit www.taracampbell.com for more stories.

Justine Chan holds an MFA in prose from the University of Washington in Seattle. She earned her BA from the University of Illinois at Urbana-Champaign in English and creative writing. Her work has appeared in *Beecher's, Booth, Poetry on Buses,* the *Breadline Anthology,* and *Midwestern Gothic,* among others. Her nonfiction was nominated for the 2016 Pushcart. She is also a singer-songwriter and busker and currently lives in Seattle.

Courtney Craggett holds a PhD in creative writing from the University of North Texas. She is the author of the forthcoming story collection *Tornado Season* (Black Lawrence Press, 2019). Her fiction appears in *The Pinch, Mid-American Review, Washington Square Review, Juked, Word*

Riot, and *Monkeybicycle,* among others. Her reviews appear in *American Microreviews* and *Interviews.* She lives and writes in Oklahoma City, where she is the artist in residence at the University of Central Oklahoma.

Krista Christensen's essays have appeared or are forthcoming in *River Teeth, Blue Earth Review, New Ohio Review, Harpur Palate,* and elsewhere. She earned an MFA from Ashland University, and has recently completed a memoir that details her struggle to find peace after a sudden hysterectomy at age thirty-two. Find her in Fairbanks, Alaska, on Facebook, or at kristachristensen.com

Helena Chung recently graduated from Johns Hopkins University with a degree in the Writing Seminars. She is currently an MFA candidate at the University of Virginia. Her poetry appears in *The Hopkins Review, DIALOGIST, The Journal,* and elsewhere.

Liz N. Clift holds an MFA in creative writing from Iowa State University. Her poetry has appeared or is forthcoming in *Rattle, Hobart, The National Poetry Review, Passages North,* and elsewhere. She lives in Colorado.

Sarah Dalton received her BA in writing from Belmont University in 2014. She currently lives in Nashville, Tennessee, where she works as a faculty assistant in the Law and Economics PhD program at Vanderbilt University.

Stevie Edwards is the founder and editor-in-chief of *Muzzle Magazine* and senior editor in book development at YesYes Books. Her first book, *Good Grief* (Write Bloody, 2012), received the Independent Publisher Book Awards Bronze in Poetry and the Devil's Kitchen Reading Award from SIU-Carbondale. Her second book, *Humanly,* was released in 2015 by Small Doggies Press, and her chapbook, *Sadness Workshop,* is forthcoming from Button Poetry. She has an MFA in poetry from Cornell University and is a PhD candidate in creative writing at University of North Texas. Her poetry is published and forthcoming in *Indiana Review, Crazyhorse, TriQuarterly, Redivider, 32 Poems, Pleiades,* and elsewhere.

Kelcey Parker Ervick is the author of *The Bitter Life of Božena Němcová* (Rose Metal Press), a hybrid work of biography, memoir, and visual art. Her previous books include *Liliane's Balcony: A Novella of Fallingwater* (Rose Metal Press) and *For Sale By Owner* (Kore Press). She teaches at Indiana University South Bend, an hour away from Michigan City Lighthouse, where Harriet Colfax kept the light for forty-three years. Details and journal entries in the story are taken from *Women Who Kept the Lights: An Illustrated History of Female Lighthouse Keepers* by Mary Louise Clifford and J. Candace Clifford.

Kallie Falandays is the author of *Dovetail Down the House* (Burnside Review Press, 2016). You can read her work in *Black Warrior Review, Day One, The Journal, CutBank,* and elsewhere. She runs Tell Tell Poetry.

Katie Young Foster grew up in the Sandhills of Nebraska. She was the 2016-17 Creative Writing Fellow at the Curb Center in Nashville, Tennessee. Her stories have appeared or are forthcoming in *The Masters Review Anthology V, Arcadia, Day One, Joyland Magazine, The Boiler Journal, The New Territory,* and elsewhere. She is the winner of *The Masters Review* 2016 Anthology contest judged by Amy Hempel, and has been recognized by DISQUIET International Literary Program in Lisbon, Portugal, and *Arcadia Magazine*'s 2016 Dead Bison Editors' Prize in Fiction. She teaches at West Texas A&M University.

Aubrey Hirsch is the author of *Why We Never Talk About Sugar.* Her stories, essays, and graphic narratives have appeared in *American Short Fiction, Black Warrior Review, The Florida Review,* the *New York Times,* and elsewhere. You can learn more about her at aubreyhirsch.com or follow her on Twitter: @aubreyhirsch.

Marya Hornbacher is an award-winning essayist and journalist and the *New York Times* bestselling author of five books. Hornbacher's work has been published in eighteen languages and appears regularly in literary and journalistic publications around the world. She was recently honored with the Annie Dillard Award in Creative Nonfiction. Her sixth book, a work of long-form journalism, will be published in 2018, and her seventh, a collection of essays, is underway.

H. K. Hummel is an assistant professor of creative writing at the University of Arkansas at Little Rock and founding editor of *Blood Orange Review*. She is the author of *Boytreebird* and *Handmade Boats*, and co-author of *Short-form Creative Writing: A Writer's Guide and Anthology* (Bloomsbury, 2018). Her poems have recently appeared in *Hudson Review*, *Flyway: Journal of Writing & Environment*, *Fourth River*, and *Iron Horse Review*. Visit her website at www.hkhummel.com.

Betsy Johnson-Miller's work has appeared or is forthcoming in *Alaska Quarterly Review*, *Prairie Schooner*, *Boulevard*, *AGNI* (online), *North American Review*, and *Salamander*.

Sarah Layden is the author of *Trip Through Your Wires*, a novel. Her short fiction appears in *Boston Review*, *PANK*, *failbetter.com*, *Stone Canoe*, and elsewhere. She teaches writing at Indiana University-Purdue University Indianapolis and the Indiana Writers Center.

Susan Lerner is a graduate of Butler's MFA in Creative Writing program. She reads for *Creative Nonfiction* and *Booth*, which also published her interview with Jonathan Franzen. Her essay "Only A Memory" was a finalist for the *Crab Orchard Review* 2016 Rafael Torch Literary Nonfiction Award. Her work has appeared in *The Rumpus*, *The Believer Logger*, *Front Porch Journal*, *Literary Mama*, and elsewhere. Follow her on Twitter: @susanlitelerner.

Kirsty Logan is a professional daydreamer. She is the author of two story collections, *A Portable Shelter* and *The Rental Heart & Other Fairytales*, and a novel, *The Gracekeepers*. She lives in Glasgow with her wife and their rescue dog. She has tattooed toes. Say hello at kirstylogan.com.

Annalise Mabe is a writer from Tampa, Florida. Her work has appeared in *Brevity*, *The Rumpus*, *The Offing*, *Columbia Journal*, *Tampa Bay Times*, and more. She holds an MFA from the University of South Florida and currently serves as a nonfiction editor for *Sweet: A Literary Confection*.

Sean Marmon is a writer and illustrator residing in Japan. He hails from Tennessee, where he studied digital media and graphic design at East Tennessee State University. This is his first publication.

M. D. Myers lives and works in Fayetteville, Arkansas, where she co-curates the Open Mouth Reading Series and attempts indoor gardening. She has received scholarships to attend the Squaw Valley Community of Writers Poetry Workshop, and her poems have appeared or are forthcoming in *The Apalachee Review* and *Sundog Lit*. She is an MFA candidate at the University of Arkansas.

Ashley Petry is a copy editor and freelance journalist. Her work has appeared in *USA Today, Conde Nast Traveler, Midwest Living, Indianapolis Monthly, AAA Home & Away*, the *Indianapolis Star*, and many other publications. She holds both an MFA and an MBA from Butler University, as well as a bachelor's degree in journalism and English from Indiana University. Her guidebook *100 Things to Do in Indianapolis Before You Die* was published in 2015 by Reedy Press. A second guidebook, *Secret Indianapolis*, is forthcoming in 2018. Find her at www.ashleypetry.com.

Erin Kate Ryan's fiction has appeared in *Glimmer Train, The Normal School, Conjunctions*, and other publications. She's a 2017 McKnight Fellow, a 2017 Minnesota Emerging Writer (Jerome Foundation), and recipient of fellowships and scholarships from the BreadLoaf Writers' Conference, Sewanee Writers' Conference, Millay Colony, and Edward Albee Foundation. Her toothbrush was once exhibited at the Minneapolis Institute for Art. She is committed to art as a force for social justice and revolution. End white supremacy. Black lives matter.

Ariane Sandford was born in Barbados and grew up in Germany, South Africa, and Washington, DC. She holds an MFA from Hamline University and now lives in Minneapolis, where she teaches at Dunwoody College of Technology. Recent poems have appeared in *Painted Bride Quarterly, Bop Dead City,* and *Paper Nautilus.* The ghosts of several beloved dogs accompany her everywhere.

Katherine Q. Stone's work has appeared in *The Los Angeles Review of Books, Fiction Magazine's Online Edition, Crack the Spine,* and other publications online and in print. Originally from North Carolina, she is currently pursuing her MFA at the City College of New York.

Natalie Louise Tombasco is a poetry candidate in the MFA program at Butler University. Her poems have appeared in the *Poydras Review* and the *minnesota review.* She lives in Staten Island, New York.

Cathy Ulrich is a writer from Montana. Her work has been published in a variety of journals. She was named a finalist for Best Small Fictions 2017 for her story in *Monkeybicycle,* "The Magician's Affair," and was named to Wigleaf's Top 50 Very Small Fictions 2017 for "When the Children Return" in *Jellyfish Review.*

Deanie Vallone is a dramaturg based in Milwaukee, Wisconsin. Her poetry, prose, and nonfiction have appeared in *The Independent, HowlRound, The Wisconsin Review, Sundog Lit, Prick of the Spindle,* and *Jumeirah Magazine.* She holds an MA in literature from St. John's College, University of Cambridge, UK, and a BA in English and creative writing from Cardinal Stritch University. When not writing or reading, she works with birds of prey.

Cady Vishniac lives and studies in Ann Arbor. Her fiction has won the contests at *New Letters, Mid-American Review, Ninth Letter, Salamander,* and *Greensboro Review,* and appears in *Glimmer Train.*

Samantha Vorwald is a fiction student in the MFA program at Butler University. Before coming to Butler, she graduated from Upper Iowa University in May 2016 with degrees in communication studies and English. She hopes to work for a literary magazine one day.

Brenna Womer is an MFA candidate at Northern Michigan University, where she teaches composition and literature and serves as an associate editor of *Passages North*. She holds an MA in English from Missouri State University and currently resides in the snowy Upper Peninsula with her pit bull, Basil; a hoard of books; and an unreasonable number of coffee mugs. Her work has appeared or is forthcoming in *The Normal School*, *DIAGRAM*, *The Pinch*, *Quarterly West*, *New Delta Review*, and elsewhere. For more of her writing, visit www.brennawomer.com.

Allison Wyss is obsessed with body modification, dismemberment, and fairy tales. Her work has appeared in *Juked*, the *Doctor T. J. Eckleburg Review*, the *Southeast Review*, *PANK Magazine*, *Sundog Lit*, and elsewhere. She teaches at the Loft Literary Center in Minneapolis. And she tweets—mostly about toddlers, writing, and resistance—as @AllisonWyss.

Tara McPherson is an artist based out of New York City. Creating art about people and their odd ways, her characters seem to exude an idealized innocence with a glimpse of hard earned wisdom in their eyes. She explores, through portraiture, the realms of our psychological states via myths, legends, astronomy, physics, nature, love, loss, childhood and good old life experience. Giving us a peek into the complexities of the human psyche through her otherwordly characters.

• TaraMcPherson.com •

CPSIA information can be obtained
at www.ICGtesting.com
Printed in the USA
LVOW05s0328010917
547156LV00012B/18/P